I0684764

THE SCALES OF NEMESIS

Larry Johnson

© 2017 Larry Johnson
All rights reserved.

ISBN: 0692912614
ISBN 13: 9780692912614
Library of Congress Control Number: 2017910341
Larry Johnson, North Little Rock, AK

CHAPTER ONE

Clark Daniels pulled into the driveway, shut off the engine and sat quietly in his car, worked up the energy to make the short walk to his front porch. This had become a common occurrence and was getting worse. It was time to call the doctor and make an appointment for a check up.

On the porch he noticed the strange orange-brown color of a manila envelope. He stopped at the top step and stared at it with both curiosity and caution, finally opened it to find an assortment of items inside, one, a newspaper clipping. Someone had been murdered, the clipping read, someone from his past. The body was found in a remote industrial area along with evidence of illicit sexual activities that, as the article stated, shocked those who knew him. Only those who failed to thoroughly know him were shocked. Clark wasn't shocked. He was a victim of Jay Blankenship.

He sat on the sofa and shuffled through the various items that brought back memories. He first encountered Jay Blankenship as a young teen at a church he attended where Jay was a youth leader. Looking back, he couldn't see any forewarning evidence of the

1

sickness that lurked inside Jay and it wasn't until the first incident that he knew what was going on, but then he was too stunned and confused to properly react. The guilt and embarrassment overrode the anger at being lured and intimidated by Jay's crafted use of words and it took him what later seemed an unreasonably long time to bring it to an end. He knew he'd not tell anyone and he knew why, at least not until he opened up at one of the meetings.

The struggle of daily survival had become too much, Clark knew he had to do something and contacted Dr. Collier for help. Certain he'd only given the name, that of Jay Blankenship, to one person, Kay Fowler, a fellow patient and participant in the program. He was as certain she'd told no one, and though he didn't intimately know her, he knew her enough to know she'd kept his secret. She too was a victim and understood.

He noticed the whiteness of his hand that clutched the papers, surprised at his lack of sorrow, only satisfaction, at this man's death. He wasn't sure if he should be sorry, because he wasn't and decided to not pursue that reasoning. What he did know was he felt freedom and maybe a bit of happiness that he'd not felt in a long time, never felt as an adult. He recalled Dr. Collier's words that Jay Blankenship had messed up his life more than he'd previously known. He wouldn't mess up any more of it and not mess up any more lives and that knowledge again flushed him with satisfaction. He inhaled deeply and smiled as he slowly released it. He no longer felt tired and instead of empty his mind was full as he contemplated this new bit of information.

In bed later than normal, the news of Jay Blankenship's death still on his mind, he felt the peacefulness of sleep coming. A thought startled him, a thought he quickly dismissed as foolish and again allowed the quietness ease over him and he's soon asleep.

"This makes a total of six." County Sheriff Wade Emerson sat with the two detectives at a diner drinking coffee. "If we count the one you suspect," he nodded to Detective Cathy Stevens, "then it's seven."

"Well," Stevens said, "there's an undeniable commonality in all seven, and for some reason I think it all started with Mullers."

"Might have," Emerson said and nodded his agreement. "All I know is this has me bumfuzzled"

"Bumfuzzled?" Detective David Hearns asked with a laugh.

Emerson smiled and said after the smiled quickly disappeared, "We have three inside the city, two in the county and the rest the State Police tied into this by MO, but all happened inside the state."

"What makes them think the perp is from here?" asked Stevens.

"They don't," admitted Emerson. "They're spreading around the load and covering all possibilities."

"We focus on the three inside the city?" said Hearns. "We touch base once a week and you keep tabs with the State."

Emerson nodded.

"That's the plan. The State will send all information as the investigation progresses, which I'll pass on to you, along with anything I have. You send me anything you get and I'll pass to the State. There's pressure to solve this in a hurry, as you can imagine."

"No doubt," Hearns said. "Seems to me whoever is doing this is not sloppy."

"Exactly," Emerson said. "This isn't a professional killer, but definitely a smart one, and one with a clear agenda."

"Yeah," Stevens said. "Killing perverts."

"But that don't make it right," Emerson said.

"Didn't say it did," Stevens said. "Just defines this person's agenda."

Emerson finished his coffee and left the diner, Hearns still sipped on his as Stevens sat and considered the new assignment.

"I think we need to dig a little deeper into Garrison Muller's past," Stevens said.

"You think the answer's there somewhere?" Hearns asked and finished off his coffee, nodded to Stevens and they both rose to leave.

"I do," she said as he laid a tip on the table and money to cover the bill. "What about that victim, the rape trial he had?"

"Might be a good place to start."

Going through past files they dug out the information needed, found the victim to be a Rhonda Burkett and the information related to her proved too dated to be of any use. The phone number didn't work and the address turned up nothing, no mention of relatives or employment, not even a Social Security number.

"Maybe I'll give Hazel a call," Stevens suggested, "She might have something of use on Burkett." Hazel was Hazel Yamasoto, attorney with the DA's office and close friend of Stevens'.

"We've got nothing here," Hearns said, nodding to the papers on the table. "Anything will help."

The call to Hazel led them to a meeting in her office.

"I remember Rhonda," Hazel said. "I have very distinct memories of that trial, most I'd like to forget."

"What do you mean?" Hearns asked.

"Just one of those times when no matter how hard you try all is working against you, a perversion of the system, twisted by power and money, and you know the guy is guilty but your hands are tied."

"What about this Rhonda Burkett?" Stevens asked.

"I hate to say anything derogatory, her being the victim, but she could've been more help, but then that's easy for me to say, not being in her shoes and all."

Stevens gave her a tell-me-more look.

"From what I can tell, prior to the incident she was a straight arrow, clean cut college student and by the time the trial came around she was sullen, unresponsive and decorated up with tatts and piercings, not being judgmental here, just the facts. But to be honest, with the lawyer Mullers had she could've come in looking like Snow White and it'd been the same ending."

"Her manner and adornments are not without explanation," Stevens said.

"No, they're not," agreed Hazel.

"So, what about her," Hearns asked, "How do we find her?"

"I looked," Hazel said. "I've nothing but the same info you've got on her."

"Did she have family at the trial?" Hearns asked.

"Hate to admit this," Hazel said, "But I'm not sure, and I'm sure I know nothing about them."

"She showed up for court alone and endured the whole process alone?" asked Stevens. "Where was her family?"

"I have no idea." Hazel said.

"Yeah." Stevens shook her head in amazement. "I was thinking out loud."

"Maybe our best bet will be to focus on the other two," Hearns suggested.

"Looks like that's our best option," Stevens said in agreement, stood and hugged Hazel. "Thanks, Hazel."

"I've not helped much I know, but if anything comes along I'll let you know."

⊷ ⊶

Kay Fowler could easily see the pain on his face, and her heart ached for him as she waited his response.

"But, it's you I love. Not sure what I have to do to prove it," Greg said.

"And I love you, and I know I'll always love you and I know this doesn't make sense to you right now. I've thought it through and this is better for you in the long run."

"The long run is not right now, and right now I just want you."

"That's not what you truly want, not what you need. Lot's of things you want and need from this marriage I can't give you and that's not fair to you."

"Like what?" he asked.

"Like children and stability."

"But you can have children and someday you may want them. Then we can have them?"

"What if I don't?"

"Then we have each other."

"You say that now, but later you begin to sense the emptiness of something I know you desperately want and you'll resent me. This is what I need as much as what you need."

"You don't want to be married to me?" His tone reflected more pride than pain.

"I don't want to do to you what being married to me will do."

"That doesn't make sense," he said, his voice tinged with anger.

"I'm sure it doesn't, not right now, might never make sense to you, I'm not sure. I don't know how to explain it where you'd easily understand."

It looked as if he was about to say something, then he stopped and appeared to make another attempt, stopped and shook his head. "So, this is non-negotiable? You've made up your mind and nothing will change it?"

Not expecting it to be put like that she didn't know what to say and mulled it over in her mind. "I'm stepping down from my position of leading the company and I think you can handle it. I know Dad likes and trusts you and will have no problem with it, not like we have a board of directors to worry about."

"I don't want a position with the company, I want you. That's all that matters, period. I can be as nonnegotiable as you."

He did have a barely noticeable grin and she struggled not to reciprocate and thought of the many laughs they'd shared and how she'd miss them and wondered now if she was making a mistake.

"Let's do this," she said. "I'll talk with Dad, set up the switch with you stepping into my role and I'll assist. This'll give you the chance to acclimate and me time to think. Just take it as it comes, one ..." She started to say one day at a time. "Just take it as it comes."

He relaxed. "Okay ..." He was going to say more but stopped and thought for a second.

"There's something you're not telling me," he stated.

"There are issues I'm dealing with, issues that have nothing to do with you."

"You've been seeing Dr. Collier for a good while now. Is that not helping?"

"Helping a lot actually. But some of the issues even she can't help me with, things I have to work through myself."

"It's not healthy to go it alone."

"For most things I'd imagine that's true, but this is an exception, at least for me, and at least for right now."

He shook his head.

"I hope you know what you doing."

"Do we ever know for sure what we're doing?"

He shrugged and said nothing.

"Anyway," she said, "I've got an appointment today, for group." She saw the weight on him.

"If it'll help, maybe I've over-reacted and this decision about you and me was wrong. Just know that I'm thinking of you."

"Don't let yourself make a mistake you'll regret," he said.

She noticed a stronger tone, threatening. She hugged him and left. She drove, thinking of something subtly hidden in that conversation. It lingered in her mind.

She arrived late for the meeting, slipped in, took a seat and noticed someone new in the group. Dr. Collier cut her eyes over at Kay who settled in the chair and smiled apologetically.

"Kay," Dr. Collier said, "We have a new member, Leslie Newman. Leslie, this is Kay Fowler."

Leslie reciprocated Kay's nod and smile.

Her mind stayed less on the proceeding of the meeting and more on Leslie Newman, waited for the upcoming story to expose the demon that had brought horror into her life and how long it'd take before she could make things right. There were no others, all the others had their demon's eliminated, and Clark's had been the last one, until now. There'd be months of gathering information on Leslie's demon and putting together a good plan.

Her mind drifted back to Garrison Mullers, her personal demon, who'd twice stolen something valuable from her. She'd trained intensively, prepared physically and mentally to do what had to be done. It never crossed her mind there'd be more, thinking she'd brought closure to that issue and realizing she did. But there were others who needed conclusions to their turmoil, others who'd never be able to do what she was capable of doing.

She remembered the ache in her heart and the renewal of that hostility when she'd sat and listened to Donna Creasy share her story and like the others she told about her demon that tormented not only the mind, but had assaulted body and soul and haunted thoughts and dreams and twisted the future away from anything resembling good. She also recalled the freedom that came later, watching them released from the grips of that demon that no longer existed.

Donna's demon was Edmund, her former husband who had a long history of abusive behavior, verbal and physical. Edmund Creasy was far worse than the typical abusive husband. Three times he'd beat her, and the last time she was hospitalized for nearly three weeks. She had to leave him, the next time he'd kill her. She remembered Donna's embarrassment at staying so long in such a bad place, being too weak to leave, too afraid of being on her own without the resources to take care of herself. Even after Donna left him he was determined to continue to deliver his personal hell into her life.

Kay was always amazed, though it lessened with each time, at how little these devils had to pay for their crimes. Edmund was sentenced to five years and spent fifteen months in prison. Though Donna had moved and tried to keep her location a secret, he eventually found her and resumed the hell.

She'd gathered and planned, waited until the right time, while Donna visited her sister in Louisiana, a visit she had to cut short when she received news of Edmund's death and had to deal with the flood of questioning concerning her possible involvement. The authorities knew she had strong motive and though eventually cleared she had to endure the accusations and suspicions.

She thought of the day it happened. Edmund was completely shocked as he realized he was living the last day of his life. It wasn't yet noon, and the day was sunny and mild, a pleasant way to spend your last day, a privilege Kay felt was too good for him. It was always the same, except for Garrison Mullers – they were weak and unable to accept what was happening. For Kay it didn't matter for what they were prepared. She had taken care of all preparations, never strung it out further than necessary and was always quick, another undeserved factor.

He came out of the bar, she was in the back seat waiting. Though she'd later wear a neoprene flaming skull biker's mask, she then wore nothing over her face. She never worried about them being able to later ID her. She knew they'd not be able and only later wore the mask to toy with them, to increase the shock at the end. The case would go unsolved and only three knew who took care of Edmund: Edmund, God and Kay Fowler.

She never tried to fool herself into thinking she was doing a divine work, one sanctioned by God, or most of society. She knew differently and never tried to imagine what she did was right, but in her mind and heart was the best of several horrible options.

If justice were done by proper means she'd not have to do these things. Those were her conclusions. But it seemed that was not going to happen so it was up to her to bring retribution and peace for these victims as she questioned why the innocent should pay while the guilty went unpunished. Even with all her reasoning she found it best not to over-think the matter. Just take care of business. That was her plan.

Soon she'd know more about Leslie, about her demon and it'd be a matter of the right time.

Carroll Grist woke hungry and it wasn't for food but for what he understood to be beyond his control, and therefore beyond his accountability or ability to stop. He never pretended to be anything but what he was: A predator. Nature was full of predators and they had their place in the system of things, but he no longer sought to justify his activities to ease any guilt or remorse since he hadn't any understanding of either. He just knew what he needed. Some need the excitement of extreme sports, some needed drugs and alcohol and others needed to push games of chance. He needed only one thing.

He set the coffeemaker, took a shower and dressed for the day, glanced at the weather while he sipped coffee. He remembered the lady was coming this morning to pick up the HP. Staying on top of business was important; his only means of income and it couldn't be jeopardized. He looked at the clock – almost a quarter until eight – the lady would be there close to nine. He had to busy himself and worked on the laptop that was brought in yesterday. Idleness was always his worst times and staying busy kept his mind off his appetites.

Absorbed with the work on the laptop, he realized someone was in the front room and correctly assumed it must be the nine o'clock pickup. He saw the child with the lady and for a fraction of a second it threw off his concentration. He gathered his composure politely greeted the lady. Grace was her name, he couldn't remember the last, and avoided looking at the child, a boy. The lady paid and the boy turned to look back as they left, watched him with fear and drew closer to his mother. He knew why the boy reacted this way and it had nothing to do with the boy's ability to magically know about his past activities, or his desired future ones. It was his appearance, and even adults would often stare. His six foot, two inch frame was intimidating enough, but his unusual facial features were what attracted attention. A long, thin face with a prominent, curved nose gave him a birdlike appearance and, due to a physically traumatic incident in his childhood, he had no hair on his body, not even eyebrows or lashes. His looks had been cruelly described by the taunting kids of his youth as alien, which was what they called him.

The mother was clueless to the reaction of her small son and Carroll knew mothers should be more aware of what was happening with their children while in public places. More than anyone, he knew this. He knew how many seconds it took to take a child and be gone. Seven.

He desired for some way to manage his hunger, not to eliminate, but to ease it. He preferred being in control. In the ordinary routines of the day it was an inconvenience, and had considered seeing a doctor in an attempt to find a medication, something that could be used to control or manipulate the hungers, but passed on that idea. It was too risky. He didn't know how to explain things to a doctor without saying too much. He'd need to endure it and accepted it as one of the trial of life of which his mother had warned. She had also said that such trials are for our improvement and should be viewed in that way, which he tried, though he thought it unreasonable.

Carroll went back to working on the laptop, knowing the man would arrive around two that afternoon to pick it up. He liked the flexibility his own business provided and couldn't imagine working for a business or company, bound by their demands and schedule. It'd be chaotic, working around his needs.

He glanced at the clock and counted the time until two o'clock. With nothing pressing beyond that, he'd then give attention to his more desperate needs.

CHAPTER TWO

Clark Daniels sat in the waiting room for his name to be called, reading a *Southern Living* magazine, unconcerned over what caused his chronic fatigue and sluggish mind, assumed it would be something minor.

He tossed the magazine when his name was called and after the typical preliminaries he and the doctor discussed his problems. Lab work was done, more test were scheduled. A month passed and now he sat in the same chair, barely seated when his name's called.

For the first time he felt a tinge of anxiety and the doctor's expression didn't help.

"I don't like delaying bad news, Clark," Dr. Simpson stated. "The tests are not what we'd hoped and it appears to be multiple myeloma, cancerous cells in the blood. Not easy to say how advanced it is right now, more test will be needed, but it's not the best of circumstance."

Clark was too absorbed in thought to respond, sat deliberating the news as he fought against an assortment of emotions. He wanted to pretend it was okay, but it didn't feel okay and he lacked the desire to pretend.

"There are things we can do," Dr. Simpson said. "We're not looking at a hopeless situation here, Clark. I wanted you to know the seriousness of it and we'll balance that with reasonable treatment and a positive mindset."

Positive mindset, thought Clark, while unsure if such would be coming soon, if it ever came.

"So ..." Clark said with hesitation, not sure he wanted to know, "What are my options?"

"We start you on a regiment of chemotherapy and monitor the results to determine a continued course. If we don't get the desired results from the chemo, then we consider a bone marrow transplant."

"What type of odds am I looking at?"

"With proper treatment, the five year survival rate is about thirty-five percent and improving as we speak. The main thing is you focus on your recovery and keep the right attitude. I'd be remiss if I told you it was going to be a piece of cake. It'll not be easy."

Clark felt despair rising in his mind and made little effort to fight it.

"How long you need before I make a decision?"

"Make a decision?" the doctor asked. "What decision?"

"The decision to take the treatments."

"Clark, these treatments will save your life."

He'd seen what the treatments did to his mother before she died at the age of fifty-nine with cancer and had developed the opinion if he ever faced cancer and had low odds he'd refuse treatment. Facing the present reality was much different than dealing with a remote possibility.

"I'd just as soon give it some thought," he said.

Dr. Simpson shrugged and appeared puzzled. "Okay, Clark. Take some time, think about it, but don't waste time."

Clark shook his head. "I want to talk with my family."

The doctor nodded his understanding. "Just don't waste too much time."

Clark drove and thought of how few people there were in his life who'd likely care about his present circumstance. His son Jimmy and daughter Jeanetta were the only two he imagined cared, but his ex-wife Jean would be only slightly affected by the news. Sensing he was slipping into a pity party he determined not to go that route and keep a better attitude about the whole thing, regardless of his choice about the treatments. Maybe there were options Dr. Simpson didn't mention, purposely or otherwise. He'd heard about other types of treatments, though he was total ignorant of what they were and would look into that.

Right now he wanted to go home, get into familiar surroundings and settle his mind.

⚖

"I can't believe they couldn't put him away for a long time," Hearns said as he sat at his desk and read through the information on Haskell Drummond. "There's plenty pointing to this guy."

Stevens shrugged. It's not the first time they'd seen this. "It happens."

"His first victim was a Sally Freeman," Hearns said. "The second was Evelyn Carter, Carter is deceased, so we need to find Sally Freeman.

"Evelyn Carter, she died from ..." Stevens began to ask when Hearns finished with an answer, "Suicide."

She shook her head in dismay. "Not hard to guess what prompted that."

Hearns didn't respond; he didn't have to.

"Drummond was found dead in his car, parked in sight of a lady's exercise place," he said. "Same type of place that Sally

15

Freeman belonged, nothing here about Evelyn Carter. Might've been his method of selection."

"Appears to be," she said. "Right out in plain sight in the middle of the day and not a soul saw what happened."

"This person is not sloppy. You got any ideas about the perp on this?"

"I think it's a woman," she said. "But to pull this off, considering the size of some of these victims, she'd have to be pretty stout. If this is the same one who took out Mullers, well, he was no weakling."

Hearns shook his head in agreement. "Not likely to be a little gal, huh?"

"Not likely."

"You think a man could've done this?"

"Sure, it's possible, maybe a relative of one of the victims, something along that line."

"Like a vendetta," he said.

"Hard to say. Doubt the killer could be related to all of the victims."

They sat quietly for a few seconds.

"What if …" Hearns began and cut it short.

"What if what?" she asked.

"I was just thinking." He paused. "I don't know, forget it. We need more information before we start jumping to conclusions."

"Sometimes that initial gut reactions is worth considering," she said. "What were you thinking?"

Hearns looked frustrated and shook his head. "I don't know, maybe this killer has some connection to all the victims, but not related. Not sure what it could be."

She shrugged.

"We got an address for Sally Freeman, and a telephone number. Think I'll give the number a shot." She had her phone out, keyed the number and waited.

"Am I speaking with Sally Freeman?" she asked.

"Yes. This is Sally Freeman."

"Mrs. Freeman, I'm Detective Cathy Stevens, with the Markham Police Department. My partner and I would like to discuss a few details about Haskell Drummond, if this would be possible … She was interrupted.

"Haskell Drummond?"

"Yes. We can come to your home if you'd like, or if you prefer you can come here."

"Why do want to talk to me about him? I've said all that could be said."

"I know," Stevens said. "But there might be something missed, something important."

"Well, if you feel the need to come, then come on."

"That would be great. The address we have is 45 Coral Drive. We should be there in about an hour, if that'll work."

"That's fine."

"Great, and thanks for seeing us."

The home was a neatly kept, white, wood siding, cottage style home. The neatness was a good sign thought Stevens as they pulled into the drive.

Sally Freeman was cheerful and friendly as she invited them in where coffee waited on the kitchen dining table and she motioned for them to sit, which they did.

"Thanks for the hospitality," Hearns said and smiled as he sipped from the coffee.

She returned the smile and nodded.

"I can't imagine what you want to know about that man," Sally said, obvious in her avoidance of saying his name. "He's dead you know."

"Yes," Stevens said. "We know, but we're investigating his death. We've never determined who killed him."

"Why do you care who killed him?" she asked as if rhetorical.

"There's been a series of killings," Hearns said. "We feel whoever killed Drummond may be connected to the others."

Sally appeared surprised and then recognition came over her face. "They all people like him?"

They knew the type of person 'him' were. "Yes, similar," Stevens said.

"Then in my opinion you're wasting taxpayers money looking for this person ... unless you're wanting to give them a medal or something." She was not smiling.

"It becomes problematic when people take such things into their own hands, mistakes are made," Hearns stated. "But, we do understand your sentiment."

Sally shrugged her unconcern. "How can I help you?"

"We're eliminating the possibility of a vendetta, or retaliatory killing."

Sally grinned. "Maybe I killed him?"

"Or maybe someone you know killed him," Stevens said without smiling.

Unaffected, Sally said, "If I could've killed him I would've, but I didn't and I think you already know that. But I don't have any children, no husband, no one that would take up such a thing."

She looked at them and then looked sad. "I suppose that's not a healthy attitude, is it? I'd never said it out loud like that before, that if I could've I would've."

"Saying you would've killed him if you could've?"

She nodded softly. "Yes, that. Not very forgiving, huh?"

"We're human and we deal these horrible situations the best we can," Stevens said. "We're certainly not going to point a condemning finger at you."

Sally smiled in appreciation. "I understand why you have to stop those kinds of killings, but I haven't a clue of any information that could be helpful. If something pops in my mind, I'll let you know. Might not hurt if you'd leave a number with me."

Hearns pulled out a card and passed it to her.

"We appreciate whatever help you can provide, but we're not asking you to go above and beyond. You've dealt with enough. Just if anything pops in your head."

She nodded. The hardness had left and was replaced with kinder eyes.

Hearns and Stevens rode in silence, each avoiding the topic of Sally Freeman's attitude that the death of these predators was a good thing. Hearns more than Stevens dealt with the same attitude and kept it inside. It was the nature of police work and the often-experienced insufficiency of the system and his inability to understand and point to the problem. He knew how hard the judges and DA's office worked, but he also knew of the many lawyers who could get Hitler off if the money was right and the many, possibly well-intentioned, human rights organizations that helped set the machinery in motion to leave the gaps that people like Haskell Drummond slipped through. These rats only needed a thin slit to allow them to return to their deeds, deeds they seemed unable to stop.

He glanced at Stevens who detected this and glanced back, gave him a weak smile and shook her head and returned her attention to driving. There has to be a way, she imagined, to make this system work better for people like Sally Freeman so they'd not be backed into these positions where they're at peace with the fact someone was out there killing predators, and that didn't help her reconcile her own feelings.

⇐+ +⇒

Jimmy Adkins was the name of Leslie Newman's demon. Kay never pushed these things and let them unfold at their own pace. It was better that way. Arousing suspicion was one thing she had to avoid and wasn't concerned that someone in the group would connect the dots. She looked around the room at each person, all of whom had their demon dealt with, all except Leslie and that would be coming. But they didn't speak openly of their demons, not in personal detail, names almost never given. Leslie was the first to state the name without provocation, but it'd take some digging to get the important stuff. It would take serious investigation to discover what only Kay presently knew, even Dr. Collier wouldn't know, couldn't know. They had a killer among them.

Jimmy Adkins, as Leslie told her story, was a guy four years older than her she'd met in a club. They dated a few times and Jimmy, as she put it, was a perfect gentleman and thoughtful and never pushed for or seemed to expect sex. Leslie stated that was probably why she had her guard down and so surprised when it happened. She wept as she moved into the story, coming to the part where Jimmy went from gentleman to demon.

There was something that bothered Kay, on top of the fact she wasn't all that fond of Leslie, who was theatrical, even her tears seemed contrived. She had to be careful, not jump to any conclusions on the matter. Everyone was different in how they expressed themselves and how they dealt with traumatic situations. Another reason, she preferred to let things play out naturally. She shouldn't compare one person with another, or even with her own incident that had been provoked and began to play out in her mind.

In the last weeks of her third year at the university, where she majored in economics and business with a minor in computer science, she looked forward to fulfilling her plans of stepping into the family business, a computer sales and service business, one in which she was already deeply involved, with a position for which she was being prepped

At a friend of a friend's party, he noticed her attentive glances and approached her, introduced himself as Garrison Mullers. He was only moderately attractive but had a confidence that caught her attention, they began a conversation and one thing led to another.

Early in their conversation she'd grown uncomfortable with minor things that pricked her mind, but not enough for alarm and politeness prevented her from simply walking away.

"Maybe it's not an accident – you and I meeting up tonight," Garrison said after learning of the family business and her plans.

"How so?" she asked.

"Well, I just bought a new computer system and I'm trying to get this thing set up. It's proving to be over my head. With you being an expert in them … "

She interrupted. "I'm not really an expert."

He laughed "You've got to know more than me."

He picked up where he'd left off.

"Maybe you could take a look at it, see what I've done wrong, if it's not a problem. I promise, just take a look at it and see if you can find something simple. Otherwise I'll get a tech to look at it."

"Well, my dad's company has techs that could take a look," she said in offer.

"That would be great. Do you mind seeing if it is something simple? I mean, knowing me I've missed something obvious. I don't want to embarrass myself." He laughed an odd laugh.

"I suppose I could," she agreed but didn't want to.

He moved on this quickly. "Great. You don't know how much I appreciate this."

He didn't want to lose the momentum. "Let's run over there now, it's not far, can't take but a few minutes. I'll bring you back here."

"Sure, no problem."

That would echo in her brain a thousand times.

They made the short drive to his parent's home, almost an estate, where he had private quarters with his own entrance. Once inside he wasted no time. He didn't have a computer system for her to look at and he moved quickly.

Barely through the door he locked it, he began the assault with precise, orchestrated movement. He's strong and she immediately sensed her vulnerability. He grabbed her by the throat and clenched the air passage. She couldn't breath.

"I'm going to let go. You don't scream. Undress and make it quick. If you fail to do exactly what I say, you will pay dearly. Don't make me do what I don't want to do."

His face was that of another person, that of an animal.

"You understand?" he asked as he slowly released the grip on her neck.

She gasped, calmed her breathing and quickly undressed, not allowing anything to enter her mind but to get this over and getting out of there. Partially numb and confused, she mentally crawled into an intense level of survival mode and knew her survival was in her hands. Otherwise, she knew, he'd kill her.

As he began the assault she intensified her focus on staying alive, waited for the perfect moment and used the planning of her escape as a distraction from what was happening. She determined her best attempt would be when his physical senses had escalated and consumed him.

She sensed he was about to enter that moment, made her move, pushed upward with all her energy, grabbed his eyes with her fingernails and drove them deep. She slammed her knee into his groin, he moaned and yelled in pain. She drew her legs up to her chest, placed them on his chest and pushed him with all available force and at the same time rolled. She jumped from the bed, ran to the door and with what seemed to be supernatural agility, turned the dead bolt lever and was outside, naked and running.

She ran across the lawn, through the open gate and out into the street. The street was residential in an area with little traffic, a white BMW stopped, and a lady in a blue sweat suit jumped out and ran to assist. She saw the lady, ran directly to the car and pleaded with her to drive her away with a combination of screams and tears. The lady, though fearful, needed no convincing and helped her into the car, took her to her home, provided clothing and called the police.

The events that transpired from this point were those of disbelief. With the money to back them and a semi-believable alibi, Garrison was acquitted of the charge of rape and assault as his family did their best to save face and Garrison used his craft of lying. He claimed consensual sex turned crazy, initiated by her, and insisted he was only keeping the lunatic off him. He did have the marks to prove the attack, as did she. It came down to whom the jury would believe. They believed him.

For the sake of public appearance the Mullers expressed their concern and offered to provide her assistance in any way needed, to which she responded with an outburst so profound it took three officers to subdue her.

Kay snapped back into the present, realized she was agitated, having brought unwanted emotions to the surface. Her attention was again with the proceedings of the group. Dr. Collier looked at her with concern, her brow furrowed. She gave the doctor a smile and it was returned with a weak one, still her brow was furrowed. Kay nervously shifted in her seat and gave forced attention to the words of James Epperson, another member of the group, as he spoke of a recent breakthrough.

She deliberated on the moment and realized that maybe she'd been using this time in the wrong way, maybe she needed help and instead of being focused on using it as a tool for gathering information she should give attention to her own needs, her own brokenness.

Clearly, she thought, I'm not as well as I pretend.

Carroll Grist rose before sunrise for the drive to Landers and was now about fifteen miles away. He loved his Subaru, respected the engineering, the best within his price range and was perfect for his trips.

The sun began to rise and caused an annoying flickering through the trees in the heavy wooded area on both sides of the road. He worried it might bring on a seizure with its strobe like effect. He felt nauseous and was relieved when the road took a northwest turn and the forest began to disappear. With the flickering annoyance gone he relaxed for the remainder of the drive.

He'd never been to Landers, a small town, but hoped to find a place to have breakfast. He preferred small, quiet diners to the fast food places and small towns tended to have those. The nausea had passed and he wasn't hungry, but knew he should eat breakfast, a habit his mother had stressed upon him since his youth.

He wasn't sure how he'd spend the day, if his time would be spent scouting or he'd get lucky. The town was listed as sixty-four miles from Markham, barely beyond his fifty-mile radius buffer zone, on order to stay a safe distance from home. Two years ago he'd driven over two hundred miles to Comford, nearly over the state line, and the day turned into a productive but busy and physically trying one. He'd not since made such a long drive and preferred to keep them around the one hundred mile mark, maybe one twenty-five at the most. He didn't keep a log or journal of his trips but could recall each one with precision, and avoided establishing a geometric pattern of activity, one that'd be noticeable on a map – just in case.

He couldn't become smug and over-confident in his planning. It'd be easy to do with his record of success. He'd seen others do it in other endeavors, become over-confident and lose their focus on what made them good, on perfecting their craft or trade and was determined this wouldn't happen to him. When he'd finally recognized and accepted his needs he knew he had to spend a long time preparing and training. Several of the first incidents had mistakes. Fortunately they weren't serious enough to lead anyone to him. As far as he knew he'd never come close to being under suspicion. All of this underlined his need to focus on not becoming over-confident and careless.

He saw a diner ahead and was pleased to see several pickup trucks, always a good sign. After the meal he'd spend time looking for antique shops, or flea markets, for additions to his collection of old medical equipment, or related items. The favorite of his collection was a kit used for 'bleeding' patients, a long rejected practice, but one that held a special interest for him.

The meal was excellent and he liked the idea of being seen in town and asked two couples at the next table about flea markets or antique shops and they gave directions to two. This would serve dual purposes, besides the obvious. This would establish his reason for being in town, if questions came up later. To date, they never did, but his practice, one taught him by his father, was to err on the side of caution.

CHAPTER THREE

"I'm so very sorry, Clark," Dr. Collier said, deeply affected by the news Clark Daniels had shared, the pain in her voice.

He gave her an oh-well look, shrugged and said nothing.

"You're going to need support during this time," she said. "Maybe you should change groups, to one with those who are going through similar situations."

"There are groups like that?"

"Yes, and it'd be helpful. I'll have Marilyn schedule you with that group for next week if you'd like." She looked hopeful.

"Sure." He paused in thought. "I know it's not your field and all, but I have a question, or maybe a problem I'd like your opinion."

"What's the problem?"

"I'm thinking, considering my situation with this cancer and all, that I'm not going to take the treatments and just ride it out, you know."

"Why do you not want to take the treatments?"

"I've seen what they do to you, I mean, if this was something caught early on and all that I might consider, but the odds are not that high."

She gave him look of sympathetic understanding and nodded.

"I'm not going to advise you on this, Clark. It'll be your decision."

"If you were me, what would you do?"

"I'll not say anymore other than I understand your reasoning, but it's still your choice."

He nodded. "Yeah, it is."

His smile told her he was handling it well.

"We'll get you set up with this new group. Regardless of your choice, it'll help."

"Thanks, Dr. Collier, really, you and this group have helped me so much."

She gave him a long hug, stepped back and looked at him with teary eyes. "Thanks, Clark. I'm pleased to hear you say that."

He stood, uncomfortable, inhaled deeply and let it out slowly. "I need to get going." He paused, looked down, and back up to her. "Guess I'll see you next week."

"Yes, you will. You take care, Clark."

He stepped outside into the early fall evening, felt a little coolness in the air and was encouraged, though he didn't know why. Little had changed in his situation.

"Hey there, Clark."

The voice surprised him, he turned and it was Kay Fowler.

"Was waiting for you to come out," she stated.

He didn't say anything, but looked at her with her questioning eyes.

"I thought maybe something was wrong and I was worried, I don't know, wondering if there was a problem."

"I'm changing groups is all."

"Why are you changing groups?"

"You want to discuss this over food? I'm running late and I'm hungry."

"Yeah, I can do that. How about the same place as last time, that okay with you?"

"Sure, I'll meet you there."

She was sitting in the booth when he walked in and joined her, food was ordered and Kay wasted no time.

"What's this about you changing groups? This group not working for you?"

"No, nothing like that, this group is great – it's helped me a lot. Just my needs are different now." He appeared as if he was going to say more, but didn't.

"How have they changed, you seemed to be doing pretty good."

"I found out I got cancer and it's not really all that good, the diagnosis and all, maybe I mean the prognosis."

"Oh wow, Clark, I hate to hear that." She felt the need to say more, but for the moment she didn't know what. "I don't know what to say, Clark."

"I know." And he did understand. He was always short of words for others at times like this. "But while we're here there's something you might find interesting."

She gave him a tell-me-more look.

"You remember when you talked to me, and asked me about that person who did that to me and all?"

"You mean Jay Blankenship?"

"Yeah, him."

"I remember, sure."

"I came home from work the other day and there was a package on my steps. I opened it up and found an article that said he was murdered."

He looked her dead in the eyes for a reaction, watched for shock, or mild surprise. There was only a trace of a smile that quickly faded and forced concern replaced it. This was close to what he expected.

"How odd is that?" she said without surprise. "Nothing lost though. Right?"

"Right. I mean, when I read the article I was surprised at how good I felt, and I thought about telling Dr. Collier about it, cause it ain't natural to feel good about someone dying. Is it?"

"Doesn't seem unnatural to me," she said. "After what he did to you."

"Yeah …"

He was interrupted when the waitress brought the food. After all was set in place he continued. "You're right, I'm not saying he didn't deserve it and all, but …" He stopped in thought to consider how to continue.

"But what?" she asked. "Don't worry about it Clark. It happened and it's done and you're free of all that. Let it go. You've carried it around too long as it is."

"You didn't do it, did you?" It came out short and simple.

This time the surprise was genuine.

"Me?" she said with a stilted laugh. "You think I killed that guy?"

She started to ask why he thought that, but decided that was the wrong direction to go. It was logical in one sense, in the sense she did ask him who the guy was and probably not many knew that information and the guy comes up dead. It was two plus two equals four.

"Okay, I see where you're going," she said. "I asked you about the guy and you told me his name and now he comes up dead and you figure I had something to do with it. Is that how you figured it?"

"Yeah, that's what I was wondering about, I mean, I can't think of anyone who knew about this guy but you and I know it don't make sense and all but you see how I could think that."

"Yeah, I do." She shook her head and smiled. "Now the surprise of you saying that has worn down a bit I have to say I'm flattered you could think that, almost appreciative."

He looked puzzled. "Flattered?"

"You know, to think a little person like me could go around doing something like this. It's like the guy who hurt me, he was killed and it could look like I might've done that, but he was a pretty big guy and went to the gym all the time. I figured it took some doing to take him down."

Clark sat and pondered over all she'd said and nodded. "You're right." He paused, in more thought. "It just added up, you know."

"Yeah, it is weird," She laughed and picked up some pizza. "But people like them you figure they got to make a lot of enemies. You gonna let the food get cold?"

He smiled and picked up a slice and bit off a large bite.

"I was sort of hoping it was you." He half mumbled with pizza in his mouth.

Another surprise she couldn't hide.

"You were hoping ..." She couldn't finish the sentence.

"Yeah, I was hoping it was you cause I was gonna ask you to help me."

"Help you? Help you do what?"

"To do the same thing."

"What do you mean do the same thing?" Kay asked after she'd pulled her thoughts together. Clark's request threw her mind awhirl.

"I'm not sure how much longer I got and all and was thinking, you know, my life has not counted for much, being messed up and all that. But I thought, you know, if I was able to at least go out doing something worthwhile I'd feel at least like I left behind something good. With Jay gone I don't know who'd I'd pick."

She couldn't absorb the thoughts that entered her brain. She wasn't prepared to reason through the idea of someone else entering the picture and wanted to end the conversation and go home. She'd reconciled all this in her mind, for herself, but having to do so for another was not something she was prepared to do.

"Clark, I don't know how you came up with this, that I'm the one killing those people and beside you don't want to get yourself all messed up and ruin the time you got left. What if you get through this, and you don't die, what would you do? You're not in a good place right now and you don't need to be talking like this and making rash decisions."

He sat, head bowed, dejected. He looked up. "So, you're not going to help me?"

"Help you? Do you hear yourself, Clark? You have any idea what you're saying right now?"

"I promise I'll not mess things up for you, if you help me. I'll distance myself so there's no way anyone can point anything at you. I promise, I'll be extremely careful."

She tried to organize her thoughts, bring the mumbled mess into order but couldn't focus. She sighed. "Look, you take a few days and let things settle down in your head and we'll talk again, in a few days, maybe a week, I don't know, I'm not thinking clearly now."

She looked at him and smiled. "You're nuts, you know that?"

He smiled back and nodded. "Yeah, I figure I am, but not nearly as nuts as you're likely to be."

She laughed aloud.

⊷⊶

"Evelyn Brewster is the last one," Stevens said. "Unless we can find Rhonda Burkett."

"To be honest," Hearns said, "I don't think we're gonna come up with much this way."

"What way?"

"Checking out these victims like this."

"Maybe not, but we need to be thorough and finish this course of investigation."

"Yeah, I know, I'm just saying."

Stevens keyed in Evelyn's number, waited, and no answer.

"Let's drive by, maybe we'll catch her at home."

They rang the bell twice and knocked once, and were about to conclude no one was home and leave when a lady much younger than they expected opened the door.

"Yes?" asked the lady who was clearly too young to be Evelyn.

"We're looking for Evelyn Brewster," stated Hearns.

"She's gone to one of her meetings, but should be back anytime."

"Are you related to her?" asked Stevens.

"I'm her daughter."

"Could you tell her we stopped by," Stevens said giving her a card. "We're with the Markham Police and have some questions for her."

"You can ask her yourself, she just got home," the lady said, nodding in the direction behind them.

A car had pulled in behind theirs and Evelyn got out of the passenger side and looked puzzled at the group on the porch. Oddly, both Hearns and Stevens noticed Sally Freeman drove the car and they looked at each other and shrugged on cue. The car drove away and Evelyn stepped up to the group.

"Is there a problem?" The visitors clearly looked like police to her.

"No," said Hearns, "No problem. My partner and I are with the Markham Police and we just need to ask you some questions."

"About what?" she asked and nodded towards the house. "Might be better if we go inside, that way the neighbors will have less to talk about." Her smile was friendly and relaxed.

They began to settle in the front room and the younger lady asked, "Would anyone like coffee?"

"That's my daughter Chrissy," Evelyn said.

"Yes, please, that'd be nice," said Stevens.

"I'd love a cup," Hearns added.

"Not me," Evelyn said, "Too late in the day for me."

Chrissy left the room and Evelyn's curiosity was too strong. "What is this about?"

"It about Henry Davis," Hearns said and immediately noticed the strain come to Evelyn's face.

"What about him?"

"We're investigating his murder."

"Why?"

It was the same sentiment as Sally Freeman's, only shorter.

"There's been several murders, all the victims fall into the same category as Davis, and we're trying to find out who's doing this."

"Someone's taken it upon themselves ..." Stevens paused, searched for the right words when Evelyn eliminated the need.

"To get rid of the garbage," stated Evelyn.

Hearns picked it up and moved into their purpose for being there. "Would you mind answering a few questions?"

"Not at all, be glad to." Her relaxed and friendly manner had returned, and Chrissy came with the coffee.

"You mind if my daughter stays in here?" she asked as Chrissy handed out the coffee.

"No, we don't mind," said Stevens, "If that's what you want."

"It is. She's been my main source of support after all that, outside my group and Dr. Collier. My husband, he couldn't take it and left."

"We're talking to the victims of these people," Hearns said, and it sounded awkward, "Trying to get information that might help us find out who's doing the killing."

"Why would you want to talk to me? I sure didn't do it, well I couldn't kill no one."

"We're not suspecting that," Hearns said. "We thought we might find out some additional information that might be helpful."

"What possible information could I provide?"

"We're not sure," Stevens said. "We've not much to go on."

"Well, it's a waste of time if you ask me," Chrissy said, then looked apologetic for the obvious impromptu statement.

"I agree," Evelyn quickly added, "But I'll answer any question you got."

"Do you have any knowledge of anyone who might be doing this?" asked Hearns.

"No, I don't and don't know why I would and if I did I'd tell you, I promise."

Hearns and Stevens was beginning to see the futility of this line of questions, with these past victims, but Stevens did have one more question.

"How do you know Sally Freeman?"

"We go to group together, she gives me a ride sometimes and sometimes I pick her up, you know, saves gas."

Stevens nodded. "What is this group?"

"People like me, who've had things happen to them. Dr. Collier is the doctor, if you need to know more about the group. All I know is that she's wonderful and the group has helped me a lot."

There's a few seconds of silence. Both Hearns and Stevens assessed this new connection, the one to this group. Stevens interrupts the silence. "We've no more questions. Thanks for being cooperative and thanks for the coffee."

"Yes," Hearns added, "Thanks for the coffee."

They didn't know how, but they knew this would be the thing that tied it all together, or at least lead to it.

Nine-year old Amy Louise Crawford was now in her sixth foster home. She sat and stared at the plate of food that sat in front of her. No one was certain her last name was actually Crawford. She wouldn't be able to say where it come from, it's a name she adopted and how she introduced herself, "Amy Louise Crawford," in her high pitched and loud voice. Loud because she's mildly deaf, and the present prescription of her glasses, that were slightly large for her small face, didn't provide her with the ability to see well. Her straight blonde hair outlined her slender and pale face. On the plus side was her high intelligence, an almost psychic ability to read people and an aggressively positive attitude.

"Amy," said Gayle, "Is there a problem with the food?"

Now in the home of Jeremy and Gayle Gilchrist, in another attempt to find a suitable foster home, she sat and stared at her plate. It wasn't the fault of the caregivers, they all meant well and did their best, but Amy Louise proved to be outside their expectations.

"My name is Amy Louise," she said politely. Not a bad or rude child, nor intentionally misbehaved, only that she was incapable of assessing her environment and adapting to social norms – that's what it said in her file. There was more written about these matters in the file, and likely a lot of it wasn't accurate or only partially so. Assessments never told the whole story, revealed the complete picture nor gave a proper solution.

"Do you think it'd be okay if we called you Amy?" asked Jeremy.

She looked at him with a concerned frown. "But my name is Amy Louise, not Amy."

"Amy Louise, is there a problem with your food?" asked Gayle with resignation.

"It doesn't look like anything I've had before and I don't know if there's anything wrong with it. I won't know until I've tried it."

Jeremy smiled. "Go ahead and try it. See if you like it."

"What is it?"

"It's a stew, made with chicken and vegetables," Gayle explained.

"Does it have onions? 'Cause I don't like onions. I was looking for onions."

"No, there are no onions."

Amy Louise spooned some of the stew, examined it carefully and put it in her mouth, tested it without removing it from the spoon. The spoon came out empty.

"It's very good," she said. "Thank you for making it."

Like their predecessors, the Gilchrist found Amy Louise to be an adorable child despite her frail appearance and assumed they'd have no trouble learning to completely love her. The possible troubles that lay ahead had nothing to do with anything dark beneath the surface, something malign in nature, only those caused by Amy Louise's inabilities that were no fault of her own. It was officially presumed these issues were possibly caused by inadequate or unique circumstances at her birth, maybe related to her birth mother's physical state or problems with the birth itself, and these were only guesses, since no one knew anything about her birth mother or where she was born. It was without explanation why no documents existed to provide information of her origins.

"You're welcome," Gayle said. "We're glad you like it."

"You don't have any other kids here?" Amy Louise asked.

"No, none other, for now," Jeremy said.

She frowned. "I guess I get a room all by myself."

"Yes," Gayle said, "You will."

"I've never had a room all by myself before. It seems like it might be scary." She looked at Gayle, the frown still present.

"It may be at first," Gayle said, "But we'll be here to help you adjust. I think once you get used to it you'll like it."

"Maybe I will, when I get used to it." The frown was gone. "Am I going to go to school?"

"Yes, you will, when it starts, which it will in about four weeks." Gayle thought about that. "I suppose we need to do some shopping for school clothes."

"I like dresses," said matter-of-factly said.

"We'll get you a dress or two, and some jeans and slacks," Gayle said and smiled with the offer.

"I don't wear jeans or slacks, I only wear dresses is all."

"You've not worn jeans or slacks?" Jeremy asked.

"No, I only wear dresses."

"Then it'd be a nice change," Jeremy said, "Being able to wear jeans."

"I don't wear jeans. I only wear dresses."

"So, you don't like wearing jeans and slacks," Gayle said. "You only like wearing dresses."

Amy Louise smiled and nodded. "Yes, I only wear dresses and I like nice pretty blouses too, but I don't like wearing brown or green, and prefer not to wear black but I will if I have to go to a funeral."

Jeremy looked at Gayle who was already looking at him and they smiled their amazement.

"Okay then," Gayle said. "Dresses and nice pretty blouses it will be."

He found nothing at the antique shop so Carroll Grist asked the man working at the register the location of the flea market, though he knew where it was. He wanted people to know where he'd been. The flea market was near the shop, likely no more than ten minutes away the man estimated and he was soon rummaging through the maze of disorganization, which he found distressing and didn't stay long. Even a flea market, he felt, could use some order.

He parked the car and locked it with the intention of walking the streets of Landers, a small town, and the downtown district appeared to be isolated to the single main street, which soon continued as a state highway. There were three traffic lights and one yellow blinking light at the far end. It was a weekday so the traffic was light and few people walked the sidewalks. He stepped into a pharmacy for the purpose of purchasing a bottle of water, remembered a few items he needed and began a search. A very short lady, on the heavy side, stepped up and asked if he needed assistance. He asked where the athlete's foot cream was and she led him to the spot. She stood as he scanned the products, he thanked her and told her he didn't need anymore help and she left. What he really needed was jock itch cream but this would put him in the vicinity. He found the cream, went to the front, disappointed a young lady was the cashier and preferred there be a man to assist him. He asked about the water and she pointed, he got the water, paid for the items and left.

He stood at the curb, waiting for a car and a truck to pass before crossing.

"Excuse me, is someone there?"

He turned and saw it was a lady, nicely dressed but casual, likely in her early fifties, average in most areas of appearance, but the cane and the dog indicated she was blind.

"Yes."

"Could I bother you for some help?" she asked.

"Possibly." He didn't like this at all. "With what do you need help?"

"Crossing the intersection."

"Is that not why you have the dog?" He wished this situation could be quickly resolved and grew antsy.

"My dog is acting odd and I'm not sure why," she said. "I thought if you'd be kind enough to escort me to the other side," she nodded in the direction, "I'd appreciate it very much."

He considered refusing and shook his head in dismay and resignation.

"I suppose I could do that for you."

"Thank you," she said and rose from the bench, the dog cowered behind her and reluctantly followed with slight resistance.

"If you'll lift your right arm a bit I'll just rest my hand there, until we reach the other side," she instructed as she felt for his arm.

He lifted his arm and met her hand as he did.

The moment she touched his arm she knew she'd made a mistake but gathered her composure and stayed by his side.

"Lavetta Elmore," she said, only making conversation to get her mind off the distress churning inside and when he said nothing in response she added, "That's my name, Lavetta Elmore."

He said nothing, until, "We're about to step up on the curb."

"Thank you," she said, stepping up.

She felt him pull away and he left without saying anything. She gathered her wits, determined where she was and tapped her way to the bench and sat down, glad to be alone with her dog Lucy.

No wonder Lucy was acting odd, she thought, the distress ebbing.

CHAPTER FOUR

"I don't see that as a coincidence," Dr. Maddie Collier said in response to being told by Detective Hearns that Evelyn Brewster was seen with Sally Freeman. "They're both patients of mine and attend the same group. They're friends."

"That's not the coincidence," Stevens said. "It's the fact we are investigating a series of murders and they both are possibly linked to it. That's the coincidence."

"I'm not following," the doctor said. "What am I missing?"

"The person who committed the crime again Evelyn was one of the victims in the series of murders," Hearns said. "As was the person who committed the crime against Sally, fact is, all the victims were those who'd previous committed sexual assault or physically abuse.

Dr. Collier studied quietly the information with a frown.

"Okay, I'm beginning to see the connection. The persons who victimized both Evelyn and Sally were killed, maybe by the same person, and you're trying to establish a link between the two."

"That's right," Stevens said. "We discussed this," she nodded to Hearns, "And think there's a possibility of the link being with this group, or in the group, maybe connected to someone in this group."

Dr. Colliers' eye grew wide. "You developed that reasoning from the coincidence of seeing Evelyn and Sally together?"

"It's a possibility we have to consider and investigate," Hearns said. "Even if it's a remote indicator, we can't miss the possibility."

"Why are you here to see me?"

"If there are two in the group, with this link, maybe there are others," Hearns said.

The frown was now more pronounced. "I don't see how I can help you without sharing private information which you know I can't and will not do."

"We know that, we just wanted to get your thoughts on something," Stevens said. "Like if you think our delving into the past of these people could be detrimental to them, causing them any problems?"

She shook her head and said, "I'm not sure. You've already talked with Sally and Evelyn. Am I correct?"

"Yes, we have."

"They've not seemed to be adversely affected or harmed by this." She paused in thought. "I can't say for sure, all the members of the groups are not all that fragile, in my opinion, but I've no way to knowing how each might react in a different, uncontrolled setting."

"I guess we need to know if you could advise us in anyway that might make this easier for them?" asked Stevens.

"I don't want to come off as uncooperative," Dr. Collier said. "I'm concerned my attachment to the investigation will contaminate my continued work with them. That's a risk I'm not willing to take, so I'll have to politely refuse any assistance."

"Could you at least provide a list of those in the group?" asked Hearns.

"No, I can't, and I hope you'll understand."

"We have means by which we can obtain that information," Stevens said.

"Unfortunately, if you're to obtain it, then you'll need to take that route. I'm sorry."

Stevens nodded her understanding. "Thanks for meeting with us. I'm sure we'll be back."

"I'm sorry it has to go this way, just like you I have standards and rules by which I do my work."

"We know that," Hearns said, "But we thought maybe ..." He ended the sentence, realizing the insinuation.

Dr. Collier picking up on the same moved away from the point. "And I hope you both have a great day."

They'd left and Dr. Collier thought about the incident from her past, when she was saved from a likely murder and a certain sexual assault. Both detectives Hearns and Stevens were involved in that case, and she was certain they didn't recognize her. The incident had been so long ago.

⟫+ +⟪

"You want to work on getting the warrant together, or stop for lunch?" asked Hearns.

"You hungry?"

"I could eat." He was hungry.

"Then let's stop for lunch."

"You hungry?"

"Not really, but I'll be no more hungrier later, so now is good."

"I envy you, not having to deal with that."

"Deal with what?"

42

"There's probably not a time of day that I can't eat, except maybe right after a meal, even then an hour later I can eat something. My appetite seems to nag me all the time."

"It's a sign of unsettled issues," she stated matter-of-factly.

"Unsettled issues? What kind of unsettled issues?"

"How could I know? They're not my issues that I've not settled."

He shook his head in amazement. "Where do you come up with all this stuff?"

"I read a lot."

"You're doing some heavy reading."

"I have trouble falling asleep, so I read."

"You know that's a sign of unsettled issues," he stated, mimicking her tone.

"Did that Dr. Collier look familiar to you?" Stevens asked. "She did to me."

"Yeah, she did, sort of, in a way."

"You do that a lot, you know?"

"Do what?"

"Answer like that."

"Like what?"

"She's either familiar or she's not familiar, but you say sort of, in a way."

"So?"

"So pick one. Familiar or not familiar."

"I'll have to lean toward not familiar."

"Then why did you say sort of, in a way?"

"Because she was familiar, sort of, in a way."

"Then why did you say you lean toward not familiar?"

"I can see why you can't sleep at night. You're too complicated."

"Too complicated? I'm not complicated. Why does wanting a concise answer to a question make me complicated?"

"Where you going? I thought we were going to eat?"

"We can eat later. Let's get that warrant out of the way, just in case there are problems."

He shook his head.

"Why are you shaking your head like that?"

He smiled. "No reason, I was just thinking about something odd."

There was no way he was going to state what that something odd was.

She cleared her throat and he knew what that meant and stopped smiling.

Warrant in possession and lunch behind them, they decided to make a trip to see Dr. Collier.

"The chili was sort of cold on my chilidog," Hearns stated. "That's why I think it's best to go eat while they're busy than when they're not."

"My food was fine and I don't see your reasoning."

"If they're busy things are set up and moving along, they're on top of their game when they're busy. When things slack off they tend to do the same. Slack off."

"I'd think it'd be the opposite. When they're busy they're most likely to miss something and when it slows down they've more time to give attention to the details."

"You'd think it'd work like that, but it doesn't."

"Did you get a memo from Grosvenor?" he asked.

"Yeah, I did. Wonder what that's about."

"Don't know, just crossed my mind and wondered if you might know what it's about."

"So, it's my fault your chili was cool on your chilidog?"

"What?"

"Because I was the one who put off having lunch, it's my fault the chili was not hot on your chili dog?"

He sighed. "Didn't say that. You're reading too much into this. And, melatonin will help."

"What?"

"Melatonin will help you with falling asleep. It works. And, it doesn't leave you groggy in the morning."

She shook her head.

"Serious, it'll help," he said.

She shrugged. "I might give it a try. Thanks."

"You're welcome."

Dr. Collier had the information ready when they arrived, but only listed the name of each patient.

"Donna Creasy, Clark Daniels, James Epperson, Kay Fowler, Leslie Newman," Hearns read from the list. "We've talked with Sally and Evelyn, those are the others."

"Then we start at the top and work down?" she asked.

"Works for me. We get phone numbers and addresses and go from there."

"Maybe we should link them to the former perps first."

"Good idea. And, determine if it happened in this area."

"Even if it didn't, the data base should be big enough."

"True," he said. "The world is getting smaller by the day."

"Unless you have to walk. Then it's the same size, maybe even larger."

He laughed and shook his head.

"I see why you were acting that way," Lavetta Elmore said to her dog Lucy. "Strange fella that man right there."

Lucy looked at her with her pale blue, understanding eyes.

Lavetta pondered on the matter a while. From his voice, she determined he was six foot tall, maybe taller, not a man to do a lot of smiling, likely had a solemn look, but not frowning. He was from the general area though not from Landers, maybe from the city, maybe Markham. She knew everyone in Landers and this guy was not a local. Being alone probably meant he had no kin here. He did stand out in one way. He wore Brut cologne and few have worn that for ages.

She didn't know why it was so important that she put to memory all this stuff about the man and tossed around the idea if she should tell someone, not that there was anything to tell and that pretty much settled the matter of telling someone. How, she imagined, could she just come out and say that she met a man that made her feel weird and that he was not from around here. Lots of peculiar folks in the world nowadays, that she knew and there were all types of weird happening. So the fact he was weird didn't point to a real problem, at least, no more stranger than the world was becoming by the day.

She stood and let her troublesome left leg get its strength. "Come on, Lucy."

Lucy was up with Lavetta and was ready to take the lead. Heelers weren't typical for guide dogs and Lucy wasn't trained, but she just knew what to do and did it and wasn't all that complicated to either Lucy or to Lavetta.

Lavetta, blind since the age of nine, was accustomed to her darkened and obscured world but having Lucy, who'd been with her for the last six years, made coping much easier. Her last dog, Elvis, was a capable animal and a great guide, but Lucy had something none of the others had and no one, not even Lavetta, could name what that was and she figured it didn't need to be named.

Lucy's reaction to the stranger was unusual. Never had she behaved in such a manner, hesitant, pulling back and possibly even afraid. The soft whine, Lavetta was certain she'd heard it, was never heard from Lucy before, and had softly pawed her leg twice, which in hindsight, Lavetta considered a warning. And it wasn't only Lucy's reaction that gave her concern, it was also her own. When her hand touched his arm the unidentifiable emanations sent her brain into a frantic whirl that took several minutes after he'd left for it to calm down.

In the early years of her blindness this sensitivity came and grew, for what reason she didn't understand but only assumed it to be a compensation for her loss of sight, but wasn't certain. It came, it grew and it was what it was – an ability to access the emotional and mental state of another, and even the innate state of their character, or as she often thought of it, their soul. These were matters she usually kept to herself, for her own use and benefit. But today was different, too profound to ignore and she wondered what could come of it. Maybe, she determined, time would tell.

She reached into her large pocket, retrieved a treat and slipped it to a waiting and appreciative Lucy.

Carroll Grist returned from his trip to Landers, paid no attention to the spectacular sunset, a sight wasted on him, devoid of the ability to appreciate such things. Once inside the garage and the door closed he'd be able to remove the child, who by now was without the energy to struggle. Even if the will existed the sedative would prevent it.

Inside the child was secured and quiet so he took the long desired shower, no hurry to finish. He replayed the encounter and abduction in his mind, looked for anything that resembled an error, errors that would point to needed adjustments in the future. The mother was preoccupied with a conversation with another lady of the similar age, both engaged in a loud and animated manner Carroll found vulgar and disturbing. The child, a girl of maybe six or seven, left to wander about aimlessly involved in anything to fill the void and distract from the boredom the mother so carelessly provided. He had the route determined, waited for several possible witnesses to meander on and then made his move. He quietly

47

entered their vicinity, the two women burst into loud laughter and he took advantage of the distraction, picked the child up, hand over mouth. The child began to struggle but was unable to make a sound as he turned the corner out of sight of the child's mother.

"Please do not scream or make a noise," he whispered to the child, "When I take off my hand do not make a noise. If you do I'll have to hurt you real bad and that's something I don't want to do. Then I'll have to hurt your mother and that would be even worse."

He saw the young teens coming in his direction, a boy and a girl. He removed his hand from the child's mouth and squeezed her arm to reinforce his warning. The child was quiet and this worked to his advantage. Why he chose those of a younger age, since older children were quicker to resist. He passed the teens that took concerned notice of him with the child. He smiled apologetically and shook his head. That was all it took as they weakly returned the smile and continued their conversation.

He'd not planned for the abduction, but they often happened like that – unexpected. The child was in the right position, the angles of sight perfect, the mother deeply preoccupied, the area mostly deserted and enabling him to take the child and be out of sight of the parent and her friend in less than one second. He'd not admit it, though he considered himself to be highly organized with the ability to put together near perfect plans, there was a part of him that preferred the spontaneity of the unexpected and quickly tossed together plans. He knew the need for such excitement was dangerous in the long run, which could put him into a compromised situation that led to detection. Still, he did like the added thrill, the added dimension.

Out of the shower and dressed, he glanced at his watch and mentally counted the time that had passed since administering the sedative. It has been four hours. He determined to wait until morning. He needed at least twelve hour to allow the sedative to clear from the bloodstream, and other possible contaminates that would harm the powerful forces the blood would provide. The blood had to be as pure as possible, from one who was innocent and healthy, only then would it provide the satisfactory results.

He'd read of those who'd practiced cannibalism and how some foolishly thought they took on the character and special traits of those whose flesh they ate. Carroll knew this was ignorance and though he understood the principle and respected what they desired, he rejected the practice as sinister and barbaric. He desired something similar, but there was a difference.

He knew that from the blood came life and life was in the blood. He'd learned this from the religion of his mother, who'd taken him to Mass where he witnessed the drinking of the blood of Christ. As he grew older, his curiosity heightened. He delved into a search for information and found plenty, carefully examined it to identify and remove contaminates of superstition, to find the hidden and buried truth that would deliver him from the flaws that incited others to stare and to taunt and ridicule, to be brought out of the darkness of his flawed existence into something better, to have the desirable and powerful spirit of innocence redeem him. It was, he knew, only from these children, in their innocence and tenderness, could he partake of the regenerating force that'd take him to the place he desired to go, to become the person he desired to become. Bit by bit, their blood and his would merge into one, passing on the needed characteristics, until the transformation was complete.

Yet, he constantly struggled against the temptation to admit it wasn't working. He was convinced two things would certainly lead to success: One was unwavering faith and the other the right donor. He needed one with the purest blood that would make all the difference. This belief drove his faith, his anticipation and his hope, that there'd be that one child who would make the difference.

⚔ ⚔

Belinda Swafford, special agent for the F.B.I., read through the reports several times and saw the similarities, enough to say it was likely committed by the same person. There were children missing and no valuable evidence to point to anyone, nothing but the commonality of the children and MO.

The missing children were all between the ages of five and seven, taken from an area of approximately four hundred square miles, most concentrated in an area of three hundred square miles. Most were girls, almost seventy percent, and nothing found to indicate they were murdered, sexually assaulted or taken for whatever reason, since nothing had been found, period – no trace, no bodies.

She knew this about the abductor: Certainly male, systematic and orderly, antisocial, intelligent and unmarried, likely never married, very hygienic, his dress would be unstylish, but very neat. Complexion pale, eyes avoiding contact with others, attractiveness could go either way, but never considered appealing.

The locations of abductions were sparse in people hanging around, plenty of cover and ease of egress. Parent, always the mother, would be distracted but in close proximity with the child, not neglectful, just distracted. A yet undetermined story was being told by why the abductor didn't take children attended by the father, since such a circumstance had likely arisen during the span of time involved, but Belinda had to give that more thought.

She'd pinned the map where the similar abductions occurred, stood back and looked at it. It didn't take long for her to pick out an obvious pattern in the locations: They surrounded a vacant area that she circled and the city of Markham was in the hub. No one knew if these abductions could be tied to a larger, national, maybe international system and at first she'd wondered why she was selected for this case, not really her forte. Either by fate or design she knew this: She had close connections in Markham: Cathy Stevens.

"David and I are right in the beginnings of a suspected serial killer investigation," said Cathy, sitting across the table from Belinda as they ate a slow lunch.

"You get the time go through the paperwork, see if any whistles are blown or bells rung."

She could've done this by email, snail mail, or by phone. But the personal interviews had a double benefit. It had been a long time since she'd spent with Cathy Stevens.

"These are children, Cathy," Belinda said. "And whoever is doing this is seriously intelligent, in a sick way, of course. You know the type, you've seen them."

Cathy shook her head, recalled the depravity of these predators. If she'd seen one of those types it was one too many. Unfortunately she wasn't sure how many it was she been cursed to know, certainly more than she wanted.

"I've not got enough to get a good start," said Belinda, "That's why I thought of you, seeing you're in the core area, here around Markham."

She paused in thought. "I'm not asking you to make this a priority, just when you have time. I've written a profile description, give it a go-over."

Cathy didn't have to ask her why she'd brought this directly to her, she knew well enough the reason why. She didn't want it lost in the shuffle, pushed to the back and forgotten. It happened, and they both knew it. The fact this involved children struck deep with them both, as it would with any good cop, man or woman.

"I'll start on this today, this evening," Cathy said. And she would. She had to fight the urge to open it up and start immediately, but she had to meet with David after lunch and needed a clear mind.

They finished lunch and chatted outside as they stood in the shade of a tree, for almost half an hour. They had so much to catch up on and not enough time. They reluctantly hugged and Belinda left town. Cathy had to meet David and was already late.

David listened as Cathy highlighted her meeting with Belinda as they drove en route to meet with James Epperson, a patient of Dr. Collier,

"Still a needle in a haystack," he said.

"Aren't they all," she said, shaking her head. "I'll make copies for you to go over. Who knows, we might get lucky."

"Luck seems to be running in short supply lately." He smiled, but it wasn't a funny smile. "Got anything set up for Clark Daniels yet?"

"No, not yet. He seems to be a stay put guy, shouldn't be a problem."

⊷⊱⊰⊶

James opened the door with a friendly smile, was open and eager to talk.

"My deal was a little like Clark's," James said, referring to Clark Daniels. "I'd just turned thirteen when it happened." Like most, James was not going into any details.

"Wasn't his name Henry?" Hearns asked.

"That was his last name, his first was James, like mine, but he went mostly by Jim. I was in the Scouts at the time and Jim was probably around nineteen, an Eagle Scout and everything."

"Did you report it?" Stevens asked.

"Not really report it but I talked with the assistant Scout leader Howard, mainly because I didn't really care for the Scoutmaster, he was a bit too serious a guy for me." He smiled as he thought about what he'd said.

"Anyway, you know, we'd go on these campouts and stuff and Jim would hang close to me, like he took a liking to me, you know, in an ordinary way. I liked Jim and it felt good to have someone like him to take interest and all."

He paused, this time his memories drew him deeper and his demeanor turned solemn.

James cleared his throat. "Well, anyhow, after stuff began to happen I couldn't make heads or tails about how to handle it, I didn't like it of course but at the same time I didn't understand how Jim would do something like that and how I could stop him and at the same time not upset him."

"You were afraid of him?" Stevens asked.

"No, not afraid of him, never was afraid, and the odd thing is I didn't want to hurt his feelings, or something like that. I didn't want him to stop being my friend but at the same time I didn't want this to continue."

"You didn't tell him, that you'd didn't like it?" asked Hearns.

"I sort of told him once that I didn't feel right about it all, and he acted like it hurt his feelings, like he thought I liked it, or should like it. He said it was his way of showing how much he liked me and asked if I liked him. Have to admit, thinking back, I was pretty confused and messed up not to do any better than I did, you know, in handling the whole thing."

"Not your fault, James," Stevens said.

"Yeah, that's what Dr. Collier says, but after it went on a bit longer I talked with Howard, the assistant leader, and he told me not to tell no one that it might give the Scout group a bad mark and cause a whole lot of trouble for our troop. He said he'd take care of it and it'd not happen anymore and it didn't."

"It stopped?"

"Yeah, and Jim steered clear of me like I was a leper and anyhow I soon left the Scouts. I got an after-school and weekend job working for my uncle at his gas station."

"How did you end up going to Dr. Collier? What brought that on?" Hearns asked.

"I was having issues with my wife at the time, you know, sexual stuff and whatnot, and one thing leads to another and we went to counseling about it and it was Dr. Collier. She set me up for this group after the wife and I finished our stuff."

"You and her still married?" Stevens asked.

"Nah, we ended it. Likely just meant to be or whatever, probably more to it than just that, you know, the sexual problems. But it turned out the group was a good thing for me, and all. I'm seeing a woman now and things are going good. I don't want to be too confident, but we may even get married on down the road."

"That's good, James," Hearns said. "Glad things have worked out like that."

"Thanks," James said with obvious sincerity.

"When did you find out about Jim Henry's death?" asked Stevens.

James sat and thought on the question for a few seconds. "I don't know, maybe three or four years ago."

"How long have you attended the group?"

He thought again. "Likely close to five years, could be a little longer, not sure, but those things can be checked out if it's important."

Stevens was about to ask as question when James asked, "Why is finding out who killed Jim so important, I mean, after all the stuff he did."

"You are aware of other incidents connected to James Henry," Stevens asked.

"I heard things, yes."

"Why didn't you come forward then, when you began to hear these things?" Hearns asked.

"Because I didn't know he'd kept it up until I knew he was dead. I didn't know if he grew up into a regular decent citizen and whatnot, but turns out he didn't and did plenty more afterwards."

"How did you find out?" Hearns asked.

"Envelope turned up here at the house and had some stuff in it telling about it all."

Hearns and Stevens exchanged knowing glances. They didn't know how and when, but knew they were on the right path to the killer.

"An envelope?" asked Stevens. "And you've no idea who sent the envelope?"

"No, did seem odd, you know, just out of the blue like that and that was then I found out Jim was dead, It said so in the newspaper clipping in the envelope."

Hearns rose, followed by Stevens. They had all they needed from James, who'd now stood and appeared disappointed.

"Thanks, James, for taking the time to talk to us," Hearns said as they shook hands.

"So y'all are trying to catch the person who killed Jim?"

"We are," Steven replied.

James shrugged, "Ok then, hope I was some help to you."

"Can't hurt," Hearns said. "You may have provided some very helpful information, at least it will point in the right direction."

James shrugged again. "Oh well," he said without conviction.

CHAPTER FIVE

They sat at the kitchen table facing one another where Gayle Gilchrist revealed her concerns to Jeremy. He's not exactly surprised by the development.

"She's just so different," said Gayle. "I mean she's sweet in that odd way, but she's so ... I can't think of the right words, emotionally flat, maybe one-dimensional."

"I don't know what you mean by one-dimensional." His tone exposed his position of challenging her on this point.

"Maybe that's not the right word, just that she seems to have no emotional depth, emotionally disconnected to us."

"She's not really any trouble," he said. "Maybe in time things will change."

"I'm no doctor but the type of things I see aren't the type you just grow out of. I'm sure she'll change some, but I don't know if I can emotionally invest myself in her, you know, without that emotional connection, emotional return."

Her tone made it clear to him that all his challenges would be, as usual, futile.

"Maybe there's a reason."

"Maybe, or probably there is, and I can't do anything about that, and neither can you. This is reality and the reality is I don't think I can do this."

She stood, her hands on her hips, being theatric in her mannerism. "And she talks to herself all the time and I have no idea what that's about."

Jeremy heard the resolve, the finality.

Amy Louise sat and read in the large overstuffed chair in the den that adjoined the kitchen. She loved the chair. It was billowy and cuddled her and had become her favorite place to read, often to simply sit. The novel she read was *Winter's Bone*, by Daniel Woodrell, until her mind slowly drifted to the conversation from the nearby room. She was now completely attuned to it and wasn't surprised at the topic. She'd heard similar and most were no more careful to spare her from overhearing. She suspected this was their way, sort of a misdirected way, of preparing her for what would soon happen.

"I'll call Mrs. Phillips and inform her of ..." Jeremy said, struggled for the right words and couldn't find them. He rose and left the room.

He saw Amy Louise sitting in the large overstuffed chair, pretending not to be aware of his presence. It bothered him, knowing she had heard, but she'd have to know sooner or later. He cleared his throat and she looked his way, saw his weak smile.

She smiled in understanding, almost inviting.

He tried to form his thoughts as he walked toward her. "Amy, did you hear us talking?" he asked.

"Amy Louise. That's my name," she adamantly stated. "Yes, I did. But it isn't necessary that you worry about it. It happens, I know. It's happened before."

He looked into this face that emitted a maturity few children have, a confidence contrary to her frail state, both physically and socially. It was a type of intelligence that couldn't be found in education or books, wasn't passed along. It came from somewhere unknown.

"I talk to myself," Amy Louise said.

"What?" Jeremy asked.

"I talk to myself," she repeated. "She said she heard me talk to myself and she didn't know what that's about."

"Oh, right, yes. She did say that."

"You can tell her I'm just talking to myself that I'm not crazy, or have a make-believe friend or hear voices from somewhere. I'm talking to myself, that's all."

"Why do you do that, talk to yourself?" It was personal curiosity.

"It helps me when I'm anxious or troubled to talk it out loud with myself."

She saw the confusion on his face.

"If you try it," she stated, "it helps."

He nodded and looked down, thought over what she'd said and felt like this might be a good time for him to talk to himself. He didn't respond. It saddened him as he began to understand for the first time she was simply surviving what must be a constant flow of very difficult circumstances. He intended to leave, but he looked back at her and she knew what he was thinking, he could tell.

"Amy Louise …" He stopped, he knew what he wanted to say but didn't know how and knew it didn't matter. Things were going to be what they were going to be.

"We'll be eating soon." He had to say something.

Amy Louise sat alone in her thoughts, planned for what was coming and decided it best to carefully pick her times in the future when she would talk things aloud with herself. She closed the book, slid off the big chair and went to her room to wait for dinner, wondered how many days she had left, staying with the Gilchrists. She'd been hopeful, but like all her hopes, had been with reservation and caution, knowing better than to waste time being sad. Maybe the next one would be the right one and the right one will be the better one.

She recalled something of an adage, something she'd heard several times in various forms: That sometimes what seemed bad at the time may work out for good. It did seem to be true as she thought back over her history, of the homes into which she'd been placed. The Brown's were better than the Howard's, but the Brown's were about the same as the Fielders, but the Nickles were better than the Browns and the Fielders, and the Hempstead's were better than the Nickles and the Gilchrists were about as nice as the Hempsteads. There appeared to her to be a logical progression toward improved circumstances and she smiled at the conclusion.

That evening at dinner, after an awkward, stumbling attempt made by Gayle to reintroduce the topic of her possible soon departure, Amy Louise took over the conversation and explained her conclusions and it seemed to give them some satisfaction and this made her happy. She could again move on with a clear slate, knowing better things were ahead.

"I can't say anything for certain, Bill," Lavetta Elmore said to City Marshall Bill Bradford as she sat in the hard straight back oak chair. Lucy sat beside her on the floor.

She'd read about the abduction of the child and that it was the same day she encounter the Brut-man.

Bill reread through the notes he'd taken and then looked up kindly at her. "I got it all down," he nodded to the notepad, "But I don't have to tell you it's not much to go on."

"Not much?" she declared with a chuckle. "It's practically worthless as for as something to go on, Bill. I just wanted you to know what happened just in case down the road things connect and what I told you might add up to something."

"I appreciate that, Lavetta," he said, tapping the notepad with the clicker end of his pen. "You never know."

He'd known her forever, since they were kids, she was two grades ahead of him in school. He remembered when he first heard about her blindness and how sad he was. Even being as young as he was he understood the gravity of it.

"How's Elaine?" she asked, referring to Bill's daughter who'd just finished her second round of treatments for leukemia.

"Seems to be doing fine, thank the Lord, we keep praying it stays like this. Poor thing is so weak she can't hardly do for herself."

"I know you probably don't want no blind woman around looking after things, but if Linda needs someone to help out in any way you tell her to give me a holler. I may be blind but Lord knows I ain't helpless. Me and Lucy can at least sit and look after things while she runs errands."

"I know you ain't helpless and I'll pass the word along to Linda. We're appreciative of the offer, really."

Lavetta smiled her acknowledgement, rose to her feet and gave her left leg time to steady. "Will be praying for Elaine ... and for you and Linda.

"Much appreciated," Bill said. "I'll tell Linda you came by and all."

She and Lucy left as Kenny, Bill's deputy, came in.

"What did Lavetta want?" Kenny asked.

"She come upon some man the day the Bailey's girl was abducted, said she'd asked the man to help her across the street and he gave her a high charged case of the willies, plus her dog acted weird."

Kenny looked to the door to which Lavetta had exited.

60

"Well I'll be," he said as he stared at the door and never questioned the implication of what'd he heard.

He turned to look to Bill. "She say anything particular about the man?"

"Just said he was likely a serious appearing fella, at least six foot, maybe more, probably neatly dressed and wore Brut."

"Wore Brut? You mean the aftershave?"

"Well, that or the cologne. They make both you know."

Kenny nodded in agreement. "Jessie wore that, but he only bought the aftershave. The other was too expensive he said."

"Heard Jessie was getting another divorce," Bill stated.

"Yeah." Kenny nodded. "He's my brother and I love him and all but the guy can't keep a woman happy. Too lazy and won't work steady."

"Your daddy was a tad like that too, wasn't he?"

Kenny looked down and sat quiet a few seconds, sighed and looked up. "That Lavetta amazes me how she gets along, being blind and all."

Bill hated he'd mentioned Kenny's dad. "She sure does." He picked up the notepad and vacantly stared at it and dropped it back on the desk. "Yep," he said. "She sure does."

"What're we gonna do with the information she give?"

"Other than if a tall man shows up in town we've not seen before and smelling like Brut I guess we keep it on file. Could be down the road it might be something."

Kenny nodded and weakly smiled, rose and headed to the door. "I'm gonna run down to the school. Be back around five."

"Stop by Selter's on the way back and get a couple of packs of copy paper. I'll cover you for it."

He waved his acknowledgement as he left.

Bill twisted in his chair and thought how he wished he'd not mentioned Kenny's daddy. Kenneth was a good man, never drank nor smoked and was a regular at church, just didn't like working much and Sue struggled to keep things together. But the boys, Kenny and Roger, both turned out fine. He grinned thinking about Roger who was about the funniest one person he ever knew.

Yep, he wished he'd not said anything about Kenny's dad.

⊷⊱ ⊰⊶

The man who walked into the front area of Carroll Gilchrist's shop was of average height and weight, casually dressed, well-groomed hair like an old-school TV preacher, and had the eyes of a gambler, though not dark but greenish blue. All other facial features where ordinary, nothing particular to catch one's attention, outside a purplish birthmark, or something similar, on the right side of his neck, like he had a permanent hickie.

He stood quiet and waited until Carroll peered around the corner without expression, disappeared and soon came out from the back.

Carroll nodded his greeting and said nothing.

"This a good time?" the man asked.

Carroll shrugged. "Yeah, it's fine. Give me a few minutes to get her ready."

"I was told to tell you that if you can work it out they need more kids."

Carroll stopped, looked incredulous at the man and shook his head in amazement. "Tell them it'll be what it is and that's it," he said without emotion, left to the back and was gone nearly ten minutes before he returned.

"Ok, you can drive around to the side," Carroll called in a loud voice to the man who said nothing and left.

In less than half an hour, the child was loaded and Arn Knotts drove off.

62

Carroll didn't like Arn but didn't know why. He avoided any conversation with him and took care of business as quickly as possible. But it worked to his advantage, having Arn come by and pick up the kids. Otherwise he had no idea what to do with them, he couldn't just take them back to their family – too risky. He wasn't going to make any waves and ruin a good thing no matter how much he disliked Arn. And, he'd wondered, what kind of man had a name like Arn? Was it short for Arnie, which was short for Arnold? Was it a Scandinavian name he'd inherited from a past relative? He didn't know, only curious, and it struck him as odd. Arn struck him as odd.

He remembered the first time he'd met Arn, when he came by with that unexpected offer after he'd contacted the agency about adopting children. He simply wanted to know how a person went about having a child adopted, if such a thing was possible, or how the adoption process worked. The call went poorly from the beginning, he regretted making it and intentionally forgot about it until Arn showed up.

The stranger cautiously entered, held the door and allowed it to slowly close. The man's eye nervously darted around and stepped to the counter that the now curious Carroll stood behind. The man looked back at the door, then to him.

"How can I help you?" Carroll asked.

"I may be out of order here," the stranger said with some hesitation, his eyes still darted around. "But would I be correct in assuming you're interested in adopting a child?"

Carroll, caught off guard, gathered his thoughts and asked, "Why would you ask that?"

"I don't know, maybe because of a phone call you'd made a while back about adopting a child." His eyes were wide with question.

"Well, this is a little personal …" He paused in thought. "How did you know that I'd made that call?"

"Don't really matter how I know. What matters is that I might be able to help you, if you're interested."

The man's head was bowed but his eyes looked upward at Carroll, who thought the man was only doing it for show and it looked foolish.

"What if it wasn't a child I wanted to adopt but a child I'd like to have adopted?"

Arn stood erect, rubbed the back of his neck and thought about what he'd heard and calculated the information. "You got a child you'd like to have adopted out?" he asked through squinty eyes.

"What if I did? How does that work?"

Arn was again in deep thought. "Tell you what, let me talk with some folks back at the," he cleared his throat, "the office and I'll get back with you."

That's where it began and one thing led to another. They offered him two thousand dollars for each child, which helped supplement his computer repair income and that reminded him he had to get busy with orders, that he was getting further behind.

As he busied himself he thought about what Arn had said about they'd like more kids, but tried to force the idea out of his head. His activities, those related to the children, wasn't about money, but the money helped and more money was tempting.

Once he took the blood from them, only one pint per child, he afterwards had no need for them. The adoption thing made his situation easier to deal with. There was no fixed amount of blood he needed to consume over any fixed period of time, at least not of which he was presently aware. He might want to research that point, one he'd overlooked, so he didn't know if he needed to find more kids.

He thought about that city of Landers and felt the need to soon return there. It had several perfect layouts for his purpose, and there was some urging inside him to go back, an urging he took as a positive thing. Might be he was on the verge of finding that one special child.

⟢ ⟡ ⟢

Arn didn't care for Birdman, the moniker he'd given Carroll Gilchrist, and was nearly certain the man didn't care for him, which probably influenced his attitude. He was a good source for kids that could bring as much as thirty thousand each, though usually more like twenty on the average, so he'd have to deal with the guy. Arn found it curiously comical thinking how Birdman would react to knowing these kids weren't adopted by solid and stable families but were simply merchandise. The growing child pornography business and sex-slave trade created a high demand, but there was no need for him to know, but he'd love to be the one to tell him.

The market for adoptable kids was there, he knew that, but the costs were higher and the risk greater. Bringing conscientious people into the picture always caused trouble and in the porn and slave business such people were non-existent. He doubted Birdman was overburdened with a conscience but he seemed like one of those twisted messed up people about who you could never tell and was no need in taking any chances.

He heard the child stirring, looked at the time on the dashboard and hoped to get back before the kid got too lively – just made things harder otherwise. What little interaction he had with kids was so out of context to reality that he couldn't decide if he'd like them in an ordinary way or not. Such thinking was a waste of time, not being able to keep a relationship with a woman going for more than a year. Whenever the topic of relationships entered his mind he always thought of Paula.

It was four years he and Paula dated, back in what seemed like another life and were engaged after she put subtle but steady pressure on him. He didn't hate the idea of being married to Paula but was uncertain if it was a good idea. What he knew of marriage he learned from his parents, and it wasn't all that appealing. Besides the fact a low paying dead end job like he had at the time seemed to be etched into his future so supporting a wife, maybe even a family, was like being condemned to life without parole; a least it was in his mind.

That's when he met Uly, who introduced him to the Clements, Mack and Eddy. They hooked him up in his present line of work and that ended whatever possible future he had with Paula, which he wrote off as history. Maybe he was sick in the head to do what this job demanded. Maybe he always had a dead and cold heart, at least all his adult life, because he didn't believe kids like him were just born sick, maybe evil. People like him had to be made, hewn out by circumstances. But he wasn't a shrink, so what did he know.

When Uly explained what was going on he knew it wasn't right, worse than just not being right, as he was sure most people would say. He'd heard everyone had a price tag on their soul and he knew what his was. Twelve percent on the sale of each kid, or whatever other unmentionable means by which profits were made. He never distrusted Mack and Eddy, an irony with a capital 'I'. They were honest as the day was long, in his mind they were. He wouldn't trust Uly no further than he could throw him, but this guy didn't matter. All that mattered was the big picture and the bottom line. He didn't know how or how much Uly was paid and it didn't bother him. He was making more money in a month as would otherwise take him six to eight to make. If things went right, and he saw no reason why they wouldn't, he'd be making more once he moved up a notch.

That's why he knew romance was not in his cards and he had no appetite for whores and knew a good woman would never get tied up with a person like him and he wouldn't blame them. He often wondered if a different kind of life was possible, like if he met the right woman and all. He figured he'd be miles ahead to just put it out of his mind.

Right now Birdman and one other freak in Mississippi were his biggest providers, along with the steady stream of the unwanted from whores and similar vermin. Crack, herion and meth numbed the whores and they could care less as to what happened. He knew he shouldn't be so judgmental, since he was no better, as some would surely agree. We all made choices and have choices to make. All he had to do was keep his connection clean and updated and the supplies stayed steady. Like any other kind of business, he knew he had to stay on top of things.

He keyed the numbers into his phone.

"I'm about ten minutes away," he said and ended the call.

The kid was starting to stir and by now he didn't care. He was ready to stick a fork in it and call this day done.

The information Kaye Fowler dug up on Jimmy Adkins, Leslie Newman's alleged assailant wasn't shaping up as she'd expected, what she found confused her. He and his brother, along with another man about the same age, had a tile business, setting floors, countertops and backsplashes, things like that. She'd pretended to be a potential customer and asked for references, checked them and it appeared they ran an efficient and ethical operation. But she knew anything could lie below the surface.

Jimmy stayed in during the week and worked long hours, but one weekend she followed him and he meet some guys, but they did nothing out of the ordinary. They drank beer and shot pool at a tavern. Another time, he and his brother met two women at a club, but that was pretty boring and ended early. She checked out his Facebook page and saw nothing but the typical drivel, but used the opportunity to troll through some of his friends and hit pay dirt with an old girlfriend, Patty, no last name available, with whom he was still on friendly terms. After a few dead ends, she found Patty, used the ruse of working for an agency, running background check for government bids.

"Jimmy's a solid guy," Patty said to Kaye without any negative vibes. "Why you want to know?"

"All connected with background checks for a government bid," Kaye lied. "They're pretty thorough these days. All B.S. if you ask me but I'm just doing my job."

Patty nodded like she understood.

"That bitch Leslie is what screwed it up with me and Jimmy. After he broke up with that skank he wanted back with me and stuff, apologized and all, but I got my pride. You know?"

Kaye nodded she did.

"Anyway, I really would've like to get back with Jimmy now since I've had some time to think things over ..." She ended like she had more to say but her thoughts carried her some place else.

"What if I told you that Leslie accused Jimmy of trying to rape her." she had Patty's attention. "What would you say to that?'

Patty's laugh seemed to have a touch of humor and a touch of disgust.

"What if I told you that Leslie is a lying bitch and can't be trusted by her own family. Her own sister like hates her guts and she ain't even on good speaking terms with her mom and dad, least that's what Jessica, that's her sister, told me. That's all second hand information. You now?"

Kaye nodded that she knew.

"So you'd say if she made that accusation she'd be lying."

"Out of both ends. Jimmy ain't like that, I tell you, and you keep searching or doing whatever it is you're doing and you'll find out that he's a solid guy, fun to be around so I never could figure out what he saw in that ... well, Leslie."

"Thanks, you've helped a lot," she said with contemplation wrinkled on her forehead. "Sound like Leslie is a can of worms you don't want to open."

"Can of something and it ain't worms." Patty grinned.

First time that happened, thought Kaye as she drove home, the whole picture flip-flopped. She concluded she'd dig a little more, and a new look at Leslie might prove interesting.

CHAPTER SIX

"It's possible every member of that group," Hearns said to Stevens and studied her for a reaction as they drove to keep an appointment with Clark Daniels, "has had their assailant disposed of."

She nodded her agreement.

"I'm becoming more convinced that the killer is hidden among that group, or connected in some way," Stevens said, shifted in her seat as the vinyl groaned. "This is no coincidence, I'm nearly certain."

Hearns knew she was getting antsy. She always did when they closed in on a case, and he hoped they weren't wrong about this.

"We've got two more besides Daniels," Hearns said. "Kaye Fowler and Leslie Newman – Newman is new to the group. Probably not her."

"This is odd," Stevens said like she was going to explain the oddity, but didn't.

"What's odd?"

"I don't know. That doctor, Dr. Collier, how she looked familiar. Remember?"

Hearns nodded he did.

"Well, I saw a picture of this Kaye Fowler and she also looks familiar, but then again maybe not."

Hearns continued to drive in silence, absorbed in his thoughts.

"What I do know," she said, "there's a lot of things connected with that group of Dr. Colliers that are beginning to bottleneck."

She looked over and he sat upright in his seat, tense, biting his lower lip. She knew he felt the same.

Standing on Clark Daniels' front porch it seemed he was slow coming to the door, since he was expecting them. When he opened they both noticed he wasn't relaxed, not nervous, but not relaxed.

Clark stepped back and opened the door farther. "Come on in and excuse the mess."

They both stepped into the small and neat living room, sparsely furnished and clean, consisting of a sofa, one over-stuffed chair, an end table next to the chair and a flat screen mounted to the wall. There were no pictures or paintings, no knickknacks anywhere.

Clark motioned to the sofa, he stood near the chair and waiting for them to sit before he did. There was no offer of coffee, or anything else; but there was the smell of coffee, most likely fresh.

"I have an idea ..." he started, but abruptly stopped. "Man, I'm sorry. I've got coffee if you'd like some." He glanced back and forth.

"Sure," Hearns said, "If it's not a problem."

"No," he assured him. "No problem at all. Fact is I brewed some knowing you were coming."

"Then I'll take a cup too," Stevens said.

"Sure," he said while getting up and added as he walked away, "I'm not used to company and all and I'm sort of out of practice."

They smiled, but said nothing.

He called out from the kitchen. "Either of you use cream or sugar?"

"Both black," Stevens said, and thought maybe his anxiety may only be his inexperience with having visitors.

Hearns was the first to sip the coffee. "Nice," he said. "Good coffee."

Clark seemed pleased. "Thanks," he said and appeared to relax.

"I started to say that I think I know what this is about, it's about Jay Blankenship and that stuff from back then."

"Yes, that's it," Hearns said. "We have a few questions for you and well be out of here."

"Sure, glad to answer any questions." He shifted in the chair and asked, "Why you looking into that, you know, that stuff with Jay Blankenship?"

"I'm not telling you what you don't already know," Stevens said, "but he was murdered and we're trying to find out who killed him."

Clark nodded like he expected it to be just that.

"Well, I guess you have to find out and all, I mean even though he was ..." he hesitated ... "I don't know, you know what he did to me and he did the same stuff to others too, you know."

"Yes, no denying that Blankenship was not a fine upstanding member of the community ..."

Hearns had started to speak when Clark interrupted, "He was a minister, you know."

"Yes, we know," said Stevens.

"But still," Clark said, "that don't make him a good man just because he's a minister. You don't really expect that sort of thing, you know, from someone like that and all."

"It'd surprise you," Hearns said. "Lot of unexpected things in this business."

"You mean in police work?" he asked.

"Yeah, in police work." Hearns moved forward on the sofa. "How did you hear about Blankenship's death?"

"I come home from work and it was, I mean, there was a large envelope on my front porch. I wasn't exactly sure what it was and all until I come up on the porch. I opened it up, there were different stuff about him and one said he was dead, you know, been murdered and everything."

"And everything?" asked Stevens.

"You know, more stuff about what he'd done to other people, but he was never arrested," he said and sat up straighter, " But one time, this is what some of that stuff said, he was asked to leave this one church and all. I suppose it was because they caught him or suspected him but no one did nothing, you know, like going to the police."

"You never went to the police," Hearns stated.

Clark bowed his head and looked back up, "No, I didn't and maybe I should've and then other stuff might not have happened to, you know, to others."

"It's possible, Mr. Daniels," Stevens said. "But don't put any blame on yourself. You're a victim and we're not here to cause you any more stress over this thing. We only need a little information."

Clark nodded he understood, having heard the same thing before.

"You don't have to call me Mr. Daniels. Clark works for me."

"How did you feel when you heard that Blankenship had been killed?" Hearns asked.

He thought about it a few seconds. "Oh, I don't know right at first exactly how I felt, sorta like I was just taking it all in and then I started to feel ..." he was silent, thought some more, "I guess you could say, and this is gonna sound bad, that I was sorta happy about it, glad maybe, I don't know." He looked with pleading eyes, wanting them to understand. "You know?"

"Yeah, Clark, we do," Hearns said. "We understand."

He appeared pleased to hear that. "We'll it was like a ton was lifted off me and I felt better'n I'd felt in a long time, maybe at anytime in my adult life, you know."

"Think carefully about this, Clark," Stevens said, "If you'd had a chance to kill Jay Blankenship, would you have done it?"

He sat, emotionless, pondering and said, "No, I couldn't do that, and, I'm telling the truth when I say this, it never crossed my mind to do that to him and never even wished it, at least not that I can remember."

Then he said something, one of those out of the blue statements that neither Stevens nor Hearns expected.

"The doctor says I might not have long to live." He said this like he was sharing ordinary, basic information.

They sat in silence, organizing their thoughts.

"The doctor said you might not have long to live?" Hearns asked.

Clark slowly nodded. "Yeah, I got cancer in my blood and I'm not sure what I'm going to do, you know, with treatments and all that, 'cause I've just found out."

"Sorry to hear that, Clark," Stevens said. "That's bad news."

"I ain't really got a handle on how to deal with it yet." He was silent, sighed and said, "I only threw that out there, you know, told you about it, so you'd know I ain't in no place to be lying and hiding stuff."

Hearns stood, and Clark followed. "Clark, we're gonna go." He shook Clark's hand. "Really am sorry about the cancer thing. They can do amazing things these days. Don't get down about it. Keep a good attitude, it'll help."

Stevens was now up and pulled out the wrinkles in her slacks, realized what she was doing and stopped. "Yes, Clark, we hope that all goes well for you, and thanks for giving us some of your time, to answer these question.

"Sure, no big deal," he said. "Hope you're successful in finding out who did that and all." He knew inside that he hoped they never found out.

They heard the insincerity and found it understandable, under the circumstances. Much like the rest, he likely felt finding the killer to these undesirables was a waste of time. Both Hearns and Stevens steadily worked to keep from adopting the same point of view.

"Let's stop for lunch," Hearns said after they'd left, "If it's not too early for you."

"Sure, I can eat." She glanced his way. "So what do you think about Daniels?"

"Don't think he did it, not Blankenship, not the others."

"Nor do I," she said as she looked out the window. "But I'm still convinced there's a connection, you know, to that group. Somewhere, there's a connection and all, you know?"

Hearns laughed. "Yeah, I know."

Clark told Kaye about the visit from the two detectives. "Maybe we should meet up and all, you know, to discuss this,"

"We can meet if you want, Clark," Kaye said. "But it's no big deal."

"But they'll be talking with you soon. Don't you think?"

"Probably will, I don't know, but that's not going to be a big deal, like I said."

"Kaye, you can come clean with me and all, I swear you've nothing to worry about from me, you know, telling anyone. I'll promise."

"I trust you, Clark, and that's not the issue. The thing is, like I said before, I've done nothing and I've nothing to hide, regardless of what you suspect."

"Do you want to meet up?" Clark asked.

"I don't mind meeting if you want to grab a bite to eat and chat, but there's no need ... hang on Clark, I've got a call."

It was almost two minutes before she come back.

"Looks like you were right, Clark," she said.

"Right about what?"

"About the detectives wanting to talk to me. That was one of them on the phone and they want to meet today so looks like I'm going be busy. Maybe you and I can hook up later, or another time."

"Sure, but like I said, you can trust me with this. Don't let yourself get caught in a bind. I can help you, I can."

Kaye laughed. "Thanks, Clark. I have to admire your stubbornness."

"Seriously, Kaye, if you got a problem, you know, even if you feel like you might have one, after talking with the detectives and all, you let me know. I can help."

"Talk to you later, Clark. If I need help I'll call." She ended the call, slowly shook her head in amazement, thinking about Clark's determination and couldn't help but smile.

Her thoughts turned to the upcoming meeting with the detectives, and how she was going to approach it. If she told them the truth it could have repercussions, point a finger in her direction and she wasn't about to do that. She contemplated and rehearsed in her mind how she could bypass the truth and not come off as evasive or like she's hiding something. It even crossed her mind that maybe it was time to put everything out on the table, to come clean and unload her burdens, though it wasn't that much of a burden. Not that she enjoyed what she did, but it did come with satisfaction, helping those shackled by the demons of their past, freeing them. She'd seen the results firsthand, in the obvious change in those she had set free, the different in their eyes, their manner. Even Clark wanted to get into the action, having experienced deliverance and wanting to bring it to someone else, to make his life count in some positive way, proving he knew this was a good thing, confirmation of her conclusion.

No, she knew, she had to come up with some sort of ruse to keep the detectives off her trail.

⊫⊣+ +⊢⊨

"Odd that we've nothing on Kaye Fowler's assailant," said Stevens to Hearns as they drove to Fowler's home.

"Maybe that can be cleared up when we get there," he suggested.'

"Yeah, maybe so. But it's odd, plus we've very little information about her past, period."

"I'll agree it's odd," Hearns said. "But not odd enough to cause any concern, at least not yet. Starting to rain."

Stevens shook her head with frustration at the lag in the case as she turned on the windshield wipers.

"You know as well as I do," she said, "that when you have one odd apple in a barrel of otherwise ordinary ones, it does ring a bell."

"I do, but I'm not jumping to conclusions."

"Who said anything about jumping to conclusions."

"I did, just now. Didn't you hear me? I said I'm not jumping to conclusion."

"I know you just said that. I meant do you think I'm jumping to conclusions?"

"That's not what you asked. You asked ..."

"I know what I asked, but I meant do you think I'm jumping to conclusions?"

"It could be interpreted that way."

"You have an aversion to answering questions with a yes or a no."

"That's not an aversion, but a choice. Yes or no responses are incomplete and lacking. I prefer to provide more in-depth information."

77

"But some questions, like the one I asked, could simply be answered with a yes or a no and anything beyond that could be considered ambiguous."

"Ambiguous?"

"Yeah, you don't know what that means?"

"Vague, unclear. How can exposition on the question make it vague and unclear."

"It means doubtful or uncertain, not vague or unclear."

"Vague and unclear can lead to doubt and uncertainty."

"Either way, I ask you a question, which was if you thought I was jumping to conclusions ..."

"No, you didn't ask that question, you ask if I thought anyone was jumping to conclusions."

"Ok. But when I asked you if you thought I was you said it could be interpreted that way, instead of answering, yes, I think you're jumping to conclusions, or, no, I don't think you're jumping to conclusions."

"No, I don't think you're jumping to conclusions, but, yes, it could be interpreted that way by someone who doesn't know you." He looked over at her and he considered the possibility he should just shut up, but continued, "I know you, and you will wait until you have sufficient evidence before you jump to any conclusions."

She tightly gripped the steering wheel.

"If I have sufficient evidence then I'll be coming to a reasonable conclusion and not jumping to anything."

"Right, I see your point now."

She glared at him, looked back to the road and shook her head.

He cleared his throat and thoroughly considered what he was about to say.

"Your point being ..." he said sounding more like a question than a statement, "...that you've not jumped to any conclusion and this whole thing with Kaye Fowler is odd but you're waiting to get all information before you come to any conclusion which will be reasonable and not jumped to."

He glanced in her direction.

Still shaking her head she asked, "What was that address again?"

"6532 Lavender Lane."

"6532 Lavender Lane?"

"Yes, it's off Rosewood Drive and we passed Rosewood maybe three streets back."

"Why didn't you say something?"

"I don't know. It didn't feel like the right time."

She pulled into a drive and backed out, maintained discipline as she shifted into drive and pushed down on the accelerator.

"There's Rosewood." He pointed.

"I see it," she said and turned right."

"You should've turned left, coming from this direction."

She pulled into a drive and backed out, maintained discipline as she shifted into drive and pushed down on the accelerator.

"There's Lavender Lane." He pointed. "Turn right."

"You can only turn right."

"I see that now. Sorry."

She laughed aloud. "You're adorable when you get all contrite."

She looked at him and smiled, pulled into the drive of the very nice house at the address of 6532 Lavender Lane.

"This is a little different from the rest of the group. This is an upscale neighborhood."

"Another oddness, huh?" he asked.

"Well, I'm not jumping to anything."

"No, I know that," he agreed as he slid out of the car.

They stood on the front porch and rang the bell as the door opened.

"Kaye Fowler?" Stevens asked.

"Yes," she said and stepped aside. "Come in, please."

Coffee and juices sat on the large round table, surrounded by a sofa, a love seat and an overstuffed chair. The interior looked professionally decorated.

Hearns sat in the chair. Stevens took the love seat and Kaye, who motioned for them to help themselves with the coffee or juices, sat on the sofa.

Hearns sipped his coffee and watched as Stevens poured what appeared to be cranberry juice. Kay sipped water.

"Like I said on the phone," Stevens said to kick things off, "we're investigating a series of deaths and we have questions related to those."

"A series of deaths?" Kaye asked with confusion.

"We've spoken with other members of the group," Hearns picked it up, "the one you're a part of, and each of the others, at least their assailants, have been murdered."

The confused look was still there. "The group that I attend, the one led by Dr. Collier, the people in that group have had their assailants murdered. Am I understanding you correctly?"

Hearns looked at Stevens.

"Yes," Stevens said. "But we have no information on you, as least concerning your assailant."

Kaye shook her head in apparent disappointment, looked down, and asked, "Did Dr. Collier supply you with this information?"

"No," Stevens said. "Our investigation led us to that group, Dr. Collier politely refused to provide information and what information we obtained was simply a list of the members of the group, which we obtained with a warrant, and nothing else."

Kaye nodded her understanding. "I see." She sat quietly for a few seconds. "So you're wondering if the person who ..." she paused "if my assailant was also murdered?"

"Yes," Hearns said.

"So, each of the other member's assailants have been killed, all of them?"

"Yes, except, for yours and Leslie Newman. We've not interviewed her yet."

"I can tell you that Leslie's assailant is living, that I know from her ..." She stopped and looked at them apologetically. "I shouldn't have said that. I'm sorry."

"What about yours, your assailant," asked Stevens. "Do you know anything about him, like if he's living or not, is he still in the area, and would you provide us with a name?"

"I've no information on this person that I could give you. Speaking solely for myself, I prefer to put things in the past and keep them there. Dr. Collier has been helpful and accepted my preference for keeping things, well, like I said, in the past."

"You can't provide a name?" Stevens asked. "It'd be helpful in our investigation."

"I could provide the name, yes, but I prefer not to."

She looked back and forth between the two detectives.

"I hope, like Dr. Collier, you'll respect my decision and I apologize if this causes any hindrance in your investigation, but this is something I need, not just want."

"No need to apologize," Hearns said. "We've been able to obtain helpful information from the others. I doubt your addition would contribute anything negative or positive. Just we have to follow through; it's what we do."

Kaye nodded. "Yes, and thank you for understanding."

"Nice home you have," Stevens said.

"Thank you, we've only lived here for, ..." she thought for a second, "almost three years."

"We?"

"Yes, my husband and I." She wished she'd not offered that opening.

"What does your husband do?" Stevens asked.

"He works in computers," she said.

"He must do very well," Stevens said and looked around.

"It's just he and I, and yes, we're blessed to have what we have." Stevens rose, followed by Kaye.

"Thank you for your time," Hearns said as he rose.

"Again, I'm sorry if I'm been overly private."

"Again," Hearns said, "No need to apologize."

"Thank you for your hospitality," Stevens said, nodded to the table.

"You're welcome."

Kaye stood on the steps leading off the porch and watched the two detectives drive away, replayed the visit and detected nothing worthy of concern.

Waiting until they'd turned the corner, Stevens said, "It's Greg."

"Greg?" Hearns questioned.

"Greg Fowler, her husband; he works in computers. He's CEO of Computer Power."

"That's a big outfit," Hearns said. "No wonder they have such a nice home in such a nice neighborhood."

"We need to turn over a few more rocks, maybe starting with Greg and their company."

"You not satisfied?"

"Not only am I not satisfied, I'm convinced we may be closer to cracking this thing."

"With this Kaye Fowler?"

"With something, or someone, very close to this Kaye Fowler. At least that's what my gut tells me."

"I'm not one to argue with your gut," Hearns said and smiled at her.

She smiled back, thought about the next step.

"I'm going back to the office and do some research. You game?"

"I am."

With very little effort they discovered that Greg Fowler was not the founder or owner of Computer Power. That would be Keith Burkett. Keith's wife was Carol and they had a daughter, Rhonda. The name sounded out in Steven's head: Rhonda Burkett, then another name: Garrison Mullers. She looked over her shoulder where he stood reading the same information. Evidently the same thing crossed Hearns' mind.

Stevens recalled when she and Hearns had been involved in Garrison Mullers' case. He'd killed an intruder in his home and was later suspected of killing nine people, whose bodies were found locked in a derelict walk-in freezer located in an old building that had once been the location of his father's dairy business. At this same location a young woman in her teens has been abducted and assaulted by Mullers and had miraculously escaped with the help of a friend. They were closing in on him when they found him dead in his apartment, murdered by an unknown assailant.

That killing was never solved.

Hearns sat down and the same scenario played in his mind because he asked, "What was the name of the girl who Mullers abducted?"

"The one he tried to kill at his father's old place?"

"Yes, that one."

Stevens typed in the file name and waited.

"Madison Diane Pless."

"What is the name of Dr. Collier?" asked Hearns. "First and middle."

Stevens went to another file but the information wasn't there, so she Googled information concerning Dr. Collier and her practice and found what she was looking for: Dr. Collier's full name was Madison Diane Collier.

"Madison Diane Collier," Stevens stated with disbelief.

"I'd put my whole years pay that her maiden name was Pless."

"Garrison Mullers victimized Rhonda Burkett, a.k.a. Kaye Fowler, and also Madison Diane Pless, now Dr. Collier, who heads the same group Fowler attends."

The incredulous tone could be heard in Stevens voice as she said those words.

"One other thing," Hearns said. "At the time I let it go because nothing could be gained by pursuing it. The guy Mullers killed in his apartment, the intruder?"

Stevens nodded to continue.

"His name was Qyntan Sellers and he'd worked at Best Buy. Rhonda Burkett, even at the time of Sellers' death, worked at the same Best Buy. So Sellers and Burkett had a connection, and both had a connection to Mullers and now Dr. Collier factors into the picture."

"We passed any possibility of coincidence a long time ago," Stevens stated and turned in her chair, looked Hearns in the eyes. "And we're no longer looking for what will crack this open cause. We just found it."

"And we need to pay some people another call, maybe starting with Kaye Fowler," Hearns said.

"How about we start with Dr. Collier," suggested Stevens.

"Works for me." Hearns couldn't contain his excitement and saw the same over Stevens.

Hearns also pushed back a strong hesitation, a foreboding, that maybe they didn't want to know what they were about to discover.

CHAPTER SEVEN

Jeremy Gilchrist slipped on his sunglasses to dull the strong glare of the sun, glanced at Amy Louise who sat erect and stared thoughtfully out the passenger side window. He didn't say anything, because there was nothing to say, at least within his abilities. Gayle wouldn't make the trip, or maybe couldn't make the trip. Either way, she wasn't along and it was up to him to return Amy Louise. It wasn't that she made the task harder, in truth, she made it easier, but he didn't like it, not for her anyway, assuming she'd been through so much in her short life. It felt like returning a rescue pet that just didn't work out. Maybe that's what they should've done, got a rescue pet, maybe a dog, and when Gayle's selfishness trumped the situation, as it so often did, then it would not be a person who suffered, but a dog. He didn't consider dogs worthy of neglect and thoughtfulness, it wasn't that at all, but a dog can't comprehend with the depth that a person could, at least that's what he assumed. But, he consoled himself, Amy Louise seemed to be a strong young lady, mature for her age and part of him was glad she was moving on to maybe, hopefully, a better place. He'd had doubts about his own capabilities as a potential father and more serious doubts about Gayle's as a mother. He knew by experience the outcome of standing in the way of Gayle's wishes and chastised himself as he counted himself as guilty in harming Amy Louise.

"Are we going to stop soon?" Amy Louise asked.

Jeremy glanced at the clock on the dashboard. 10:43.

"Yes, we can stop anytime you'd like. Are you hungry?"

"I'm not very hungry, not right now."

"You need to use the restroom?"

"No, I don't."

"Why did you ask if we are stopping soon?"

"I wanted to know if we are stopping soon, that's all, or if we're going to drive all the way without stopping."

"I think we should stop, maybe for lunch, to eat and to rest. Sort of a long drive to make without stopping."

She nodded she agreed.

"I wonder if LeAnn is still there?"

"Huh?"

"I'm sorry, I was speaking to myself. I wondered if LeAnn is still there, at the home."

"Oh, okay," he said. "LeAnn a friend of yours?"

"No, she's not a friend and makes fun of me and that's why I wondered if she was still there."

"That's not nice at all," he said looking thoughtfully at her.

She glanced to him, sighed and said, almost scolding in tone, "I know that's not nice otherwise I'd be her friend." She shook her head in amazement and looked back out the window. "I tried to be her friend. I tried very hard but she is too mad to be friends with anyone."

"Why is she so mad?"

"Because of all the people who have hurt her is why she is so mad and she's mad at everyone, even those who try to be nice to her. I did, and Mrs. Niles tried hard, maybe harder than me to be nice to her, but she was just too mad."

Jeremy only thought he had insight into this girl.

"It's nice of you to try, to try to be her friend, even if she won't let you."

Amy Louise continued to look out the window.

"I will try more, if she's still there and I know she is because no one … well, she won't let anyone be nice to her and nobody wants a kid like that. Do they?"

Amy Louise turned to look at Jeremy.

He hesitated in his answer and thought it over. "No, they wouldn't."

The realization of his words swarmed as he thought no one would want a kid like that, and he was taking her back because she too was a kid that nobody wanted. She wasn't mean and angry, but thoughtful and polite and had a calmness he'd rarely, if ever, seen. Why was the world so cruel at times and why did he imagine he was now a player in one of those cruel acts?

"Don't blame yourself, Mr. Gilchrist. It's not your fault, I know that and it's okay, really it is."

He wondered how she could know what he was thinking. He couldn't look at her, not right now, and if he did he knew he'd cry and he didn't want to cry. He didn't like to cry and it wouldn't solve anything, it never did. He had to be strong, like the man his dad said he had to be. But, he didn't feel strong and only knew he sat across from someone who epitomized strength and he didn't come close to comprehending it.

"When we stop can I get a cheeseburger with extra cheese and no mayonnaise and with mustard, pickles and tomato and no lettuce?"

"You sure can, Amy Louise," he said overwhelmed with relief at the change in topic and sighed as the tension slipped away. "That sounds so good think I'll have one just like it."

They rode in silence for some time before he had the courage to look at her and she sat looking straight ahead, erect and serene, she glanced his way and suppressed a smile as she refocused directly ahead.

He shook his head and marveled at this young lady and saddened at the thought she was about to leave his life forever. It would be less rich because of it. His brain scrambled to imagine a plan, a way to make it all work out where she could stay.

No, he knew differently. He knew Gayle too well.

Jeremy stood in hesitation, having no reason to stay and no urge to go, hoping for some rescue to his dilemma of having Amy Louise permanently gone from his life. He had to go, no rescue coming, so he shook hands with Mrs. Niles and gave Amy Louise a tiny wave, knowing he didn't have the emotional strength to hug her. Then he left.

"Hope you don't mind," said Mrs. Niles, who wasn't married but widowed, "you'll have to bunk in a different room from the one you had."

"I don't mind," she said with calm, "not at all."

"LeAnn is still here," she said matter-of-factly.

Amy Louise looked at Mrs. Niles. "And she'll be in the room I'm bunking in."

"Exactly," she smiled and winked.

"Is LeAnn still ... uh, you know?"

"I'm afraid she is. But, the good news is she's not a worse Leann, but the same one."

Amy Louise nodded with a smirk. "That's okay. No problem."

"Didn't think it would be. And, by the way, that's a very pretty blouse and skirt you have there."

"Yes, it is very pretty. Mrs. Gilchrist bought it for me." She lightly rubbed the fabric of the skirt. "This is a very pretty blue, don't you think so?"

"My favorite of all colors, blue, and that's about as pretty a blue as I've seen."

Mrs. Niles stooped down and looked Amy Louise in her eyes. "Now you don't worry about what will be and what was. Tomorrow is another day and who knows what will happen. Right?"

"Right," she said and smiled broadly, loving Mrs. Niles and her optimistic ways. "And you don't worry about me cause I know something good is going to happen and I figured it all out."

"You figured it out?"

"I did. I was thinking, after I heard Mrs. Gilchrist said she didn't want me to stay there anymore, that each time things improve a little bit at a time and I think that very soon something good is going to happen and I'll find the right place to be and I'll be there for good."

Mrs. Niles thought that Amy Louise never ceased to amaze.

"We'll get your things put away and you can rest a while. We'll be eating soon. Take that small bag with you and we'll get the others."

She picked up the small bag and walked the hallway to the room, set her bag inside the door, to the side. She went to find the others, knowing where they'd be this time of day.

LeAnn and Amy Louise made eye contact at the same time and LeAnn quickly looked away as Paul stepped up.

"You come back," Paul stated. "What happened?"

"You know what happened."

Paul nodded he did. "I had an operation while you were gone."

She looked him up and down. "What kind of operation?"

"Pendicitis."

"Did it hurt?"

"Naw, it didn't hurt. It was nothing and they didn't pop, just regular pendicitis, so it was nothing."

"Good that you're alright now."

"You alright?"

"Sure, I'm alright." She glanced around. "Where's Melissa?"

"She ain't here any more."

"She get fostered or adopted?"

"Don't know what happened but wasn't adopted or fostered. Something got fixed with her parents and she went back with them or something like that, I don't know what happened."

Amy Louise nodded she understood. "Hope that's a good thing for Melissa."

He nodded his agreement. "Well, one thing I know for me is that my parents ain't never going to get fixed up where I can go with them."

She knew his parents died after his birth and didn't say or acknowledge anything about that. "That makes two of us."

Amy Louise walked away and Paul followed until he realized she was walking towards LeAnn and veered away.

"Hi," Amy Louise said.

LeAnn frowned and stared, then, "So they brought you back?"

She nodded they did. "You okay?"

"Do I look like I'm okay? How can you be okay and be in this stupid place with all these stupid people and now you are back. Just one more to deal with."

"I learned something while I was gone."

"Who cares?"

Amy Louise gently placed her hand on LeAnn's arm and she immediately snatched it back.

She gazed at her with great curiosity. "Why did you touch me like that? You don't touch me like that."

Amy Louise again placed her hand on LeAnn's arm. It wasn't snatched back but slowly pulled it away.

"I said don't touch me like that," LeAnn said without conviction.

"You and I are going to be friends," Amy Louise said with conviction.

LeAnn frowned and chuckled. "You and I are going to be friends? You can't just say that, like that out of the blue. How can you just say that?"

"Because it's true. You and I are going to be friends. We're already friends it's just you don't know it."

She laughed, trying to be convincing. "Where did you come up with that? That's not what you learned while you were gone, is it? Cause if it is, it's stupid. You know that don't you?"

"No, that's not what I learned while I was gone, but it's something I learned just a few minutes ago and it's true that you and I are going to be friends and ..." She dropped the sentence.

"And what?" asked LeAnn.

"And you may as well get used to." She smiled and walked away, stopped and looked back. "When you get time could you show me which bed I can use?"

"You're not rooming with us are you?"

"Yes, I am, at least for now." She thought for a second. "Which will work out great since you and I are going to be friends."

"Let's get it over with," LeAnn said with feigned disgust, shaking her head. "And don't get your tiny little heart all set on us being friends."

Walking side by side, down the hallway to the room, Leann looked at Amy Louise, looked her up and down. "You and those stupid blouses and skirts."

Amy Louise smiled with satisfaction.

⥤+ +⥢

"It's no problem, me being gone from the home," said Raynetta Niles to her sister Lavetta Elmore, "There's nothing to worry about

91

with Eddie and Rachelle. They can handle everything. Besides it's been, what, about six weeks since I been to see you?"

"One of these days I'm gonna take you up on the offer and move up that way," Lavetta said. "But right now me and Lucy got things under control."

"You might want to consider that and the sooner the better while you're health is good and all."

"Nothing wrong with my health and besides, your the oldest and if anyone ought to be concerned about their health it'll be you, not me. Being blind doesn't drag the rest of me down, you know?"

"I know how stubborn ..."

Lavetta interrupted, "It's called independent, not stubborn."

"Okay then. I know how independent you are and how important it is and you know I'm not going to baby you like a helpless invalid. Fact is, you'd be some help and take some off me. I might come closer to working you to death than throwing you some slack."

"I suspected as much." Lavetta laughed and paused a second, looked at Raynetta with concern. "So, you are doing alright?"

"I am, thank the Lord above for that." She said and raised her hand upward. "Oh, you know that girl I've told you about, Amy Louise? She's back."

"Another one, huh?"

"Yeah," she said. "Don't know what's into folks nowadays, they think life has to be rosy and easy. The least little bend in the road and they get all out of whack."

"Don't they though. How's she doing, Amy Louise?"

"She seems in good spirit, fact is, and listen to this, she told me she thought all this was working out for something good and she'd figured it out. Ain't that something, a girl her age and saying things like that?"

"Who knows, maybe something good is about to happen for the girl. Not like it ain't about time."

"That's the truth. Poor thing been shuffled back and forth like nobody's business. I'm amazed she takes it like she does. Like what I just told you, about her attitude about all that."

"There's a good about most all things. Like me going blind. Good come of it, you know.

Raynetta nodded she did know but realized she didn't. "What good come of the blindness?"

"I don't have to divert my eyes to try and not look at the big' ol' warty thing on Aunt Della's forehead."

Raynetta busted out laughing. "You know," she said in a high, laughing pitch, "with her money and all they can do you'd think she'd have that thing taken off."

"It was a sight to look at, I tell ya."

"Still is," Raynetta said with laughter.

"Don't let me forget," Lavetta said, "I need you to drop me off at Lancaster's, save me some walking."

"Might as well go now. I've got to get headed back that way."

"Let me put Lucy's leash on and I'll be ready to go."

"Don't you think it'd be safer to use a harness like you did with Elvis?" she asked while stretching her way up and leaning back to loosen her back that had grown stiff. "This getting old ain't for the faint of heart."

"Don't need it with Lucy. She's different, not like any dog I ever knew." She looked at Lucy and winked, who had turn when she heard her name. "You don't go getting the big head."

Lucy responded with a yawn, a tail wag, stood, stretched and shook all over.

They pulled to the curb next to the store. Lucy hopped out as soon as Raynetta opened the door, stood beside the door and waited for Lavetta, who was soon out, getting her bearings while she gave her left leg time to strengthen.

"You take care, Sis. You call me if you need anything and don't worry about being a bother cause you can't be."

"Thanks," she said, waving her off. "I'm fine. You go. Love you and drive safe."

Inside the store, she and Lucy maneuvered their way to the bench.

They'd not more than settled in when Jack showed up. "Afternoon, Lavetta. What can we get for you today?"

"Just a few things I'm running short of," she said and handed him the list.

"We'll get that for ya. Won't take but a minute or two."

He was off in a flash. She liked Jack, and it was nice of him to do what he did for her. It did bothered her he never said anything to Lucy, not even a word. He didn't have to do what he did, run these little errands for her, but then she did buy a big ticket of items once of month that they delivered. Josh, the boy who brought the groceries and stuff, he was a good kid, did more than he had to and always took notice of Lucy. All in all she wasn't going to hold it against Jack. He might've had a traumatic incident with a dog when he was a kid, or something like that, so she'd give him the benefit of the doubt. She didn't trust folks who just for no reason didn't like dogs, but she knew Jack was a good man else he'd not be manager of Lancaster's. But then he was married to Mike Lancaster's daughter, so who knows.

"Hello, Lavetta." She knew the voice belonged to Linda Bradford. "How you and Lucy doing today?"

"We're doing extra special today. Raynetta came down, spent some time. Was real nice."

"How she doing?"

"She's doing very good. Busy. But you know how she is, loves to be busy. How's Elaine?"

"I'm fine," came the small voice.

"Well I swear you standing over their like a ghost and good to hear you're doing fine."

94

"Bill said you come by the office a while back and said you offered to help. I wanted to say how I appreciated your offer. It was nice of you to do that."

"I meant it, every bit of it. Some things I can do that can be helpful, I'm sure. Like to feel like I'm being helpful."

"You're more help to folks than you can imagine, Lavetta Elmore," Linda declared. "You're a person to inspire others, a person of wisdom too, and faith more than you see in most people …"

"You best stop right there before Lucy gets the idea I'm getting too big headed."

"Well, shoot, you are and that's God's truth"

There was a pocket of silence.

"Lavetta, knowing you're a woman of faith, and how you pray for Elaine and all and we appreciate that. Bill and I are considering getting a child. Would you help us pray about that?"

"What do you mean getting a child, like adopting one?"

"Yes, most likely that's what we'll do. With Elaine doing so well now we thought this was a good thing to do."

Lavetta knew that Linda couldn't have children. Elaine was adopted as an infant. She also knew that Elaine was not doing as well as they'd hoped and prayed for. Not in any imminent crisis, but not good. So, this new development puzzled her.

"Well you know I'll be praying you and Bill make the right decision and it all works out fine for you."

"Got your items together." It was Jack.

"Thanks, Jack," she said and knew he'd set the small package on the bench.

"Why don't you let me take you home," Linda offered. "We're done and are headed out."

"Not gonna turn down the offer and I'm highly obliged, me and Lucy both."

Lavetta rode up front with Linda, Elaine sat in the back with Lucy and they played with one another the entire trip. Lavetta sensed Elaine to be a great soul with a huge heart and figured some of that came due to her struggle. She found it unbearable that the sickness would win out and refused to accept it and determined to pray the harder. The Lord just had to be merciful in this and see to it that Elaine would be fine. He just had to.

It was while Lavetta prepared her meal that evening that it came to her. Here it was that Bill and Linda wanted a child and at the same time Raynetta tells her about Amy Louise coming back. She'd never met the girl, but knew from Raynetta she was extraordinarily special in, as Raynetta put it, an indefinable way. Maybe, she thought, just maybe all this lined up like it was no accident, but she reigned in her thoughts. She had to be careful and not become too intrusive, after all, for some reason Amy Louise kept coming back and maybe Bill and Linda didn't need that. But it did seem right, things lining up like they did. She'd pray about it and see how things went, might even drop the notion to Bill and see how that settled in.

It was three days later her chance came.

"Hey there, Lavetta." It was Bill Bradford.

She and Lucy sat in one of their regular spots, a bench inside the tiny city park.

"Hey there back, Bill. What brings you by? You here to arrest me?"

He sat beside her. "You need arresting?"

"Just sitting here pondering and I got my license, so you can't get me for pondering without a license and if I'm pondering I'm not actually loitering and so you can't get me for that either."

"Looks like you're in the clear this time. What about Lucy, she up to no good?"

"That might be a different story. You know how she is, always up to some kind of trouble."

"Linda said she ran into you at Lancaster's."

"Yeah, she did, her and Elaine. Said something about you maybe looking into getting a child."

"Yeah, but I wasn't completely sold on the idea, with Elaine not doing as good as what we'd hope for."

"That's what I was wondering, if you don't mind me wondering into your business, but it puzzled me."

"Yeah, did me too, at first, cause Linda's thinking was having someone new around, a young kid, as we'd decided not to go with an infant like we did with Elaine, might bring some spark, make some sort of difference. Not sure I can explain."

"Think I know what you mean, and while we're on the topic, there's something I want to pass this along to you." She hesitated until she knew how to enter the subject. "Raynetta, over at the home, has this one girl, such a special girl too, that I was hoping, maybe more wondering, if you and Linda might give some consideration to maybe visiting the place, to see the girl. I could sit and try to explain all day long but you won't understand until you meet the girl."

Bill sat quietly for a bit. "I'll speak to Linda about it, see what she says and might give you a holler later on, if she's interested."

"Won't hurt to meet the girl, least you can do that."

"You feel strong about this." It was a statement, not a question.

"Don't want to be pressing something on you and Linda, not that at all, but I do think it might be good if you and her run over and meet the girl." Lavetta laughed. "Best I can tell she's got an oddness about her, but she's polite, sweet and, well just plain special is all I can say. That's what Raynetta says too, just plain special."

"What do you mean by oddness?"

"Not a bad oddness, but she's not like most kids, maybe not like any other kid. Like I said, maybe you could meet her, talk with her some, and if you do it might be good if you take Elaine along. Might be the right thing to do, taking her along."

Bill again sat quiet for a bit.

"I'll talk to Linda. Right now I got run along."

"Anything on the missing girl?" asked Lavetta.

"Nothing," he said. "You know, she was taken not far from here." He pointed in the direction. "Sadly, her mom isn't doing well. Blames herself. At least that's what I heard."

"Just a horrible, horrible thing. What's wrong with this world, Bill?"

Bill shook his head, looking down. "Don't know, Lavetta, don't know. We should be thankful, here in Landers, not as bad as lots of places."

"That's true, but one taken child is bad enough."

"Sure is," he said, rose from the bench. "Take care, Lavetta. I'll be in touch."

"You take care yourself."

She sat for a while longer, got up, gave the leg time to catch up and she and Lucy headed home. It was a lovely evening, she thought, and must be partly cloudy, but the wind felt good. She thought of that girl, Amy Louise, and wondered if Bill and Linda would go meet her. It might be good, regardless of what Bill did, to meet the girl herself. She decided to do just that.

CHAPTER EIGHT

Dr. Collier sounded reluctant, maybe irritated, when Stevens called to set up another interview related to the serial killings. Maybe, she considered, she's having a bad day.

She and Hearns arrived early and whatever Stevens had thought she'd detected on the phone was now gone. Either that or she'd been mistaken.

"Hate to bother you again." Stevens jumped right into the subject. "But we've discovered new details on the case and thought we'd start with you."

Dr. Collier gave them a concerned, please-continue look.

"Are you aware that the person who abducted and assaulted Kaye Fowler is the same person who abducted and assaulted you?"

The look on her face told them she didn't.

"No …" she said trailing off into her thoughts as she tried to bring sense to the words she'd heard.

"At the time of the assault she went by the name of Rhonda Burkett," Hearns said. "Burkett is her maiden name and Rhonda her first."

"That name means nothing," Dr. Collier said.

"Also, prior to Mullers death he killed an intruder in his home," Stevens said. "After further investigation into the victim, a man named Qyntan Sellers, we found a connection between you and him."

Dr. Collier scooted back into her seat, deflated in amazement. "To me?"

"Yes, though indirectly. He worked at Lowes. Isn't your dad employed there?

"Yes, or he was. He's retired now."

Hearns placed a picture of Sellers on the coffee table and slid it to her.

"This is a high school picture of him. You recognized him?"

Even before she lifted the picture she knew who it was and the recognition must've been obvious on her face.

"You know him?" asked Stevens.

"Yes, I mean, no, I don't know him, but he stalked me once."

Stevens looked to Hearns with raised eyebrows.

"Explain what happened, when he stalked you," Hearns said.

"Maybe I shouldn't have said he stalked me since I'm not totally sure he did, but it was either that or a lot of strange coincidences."

"But you're certain you've met this man?" Stevens asked, nodding to the picture.

"Well, I've encountered this person, only briefly, not officially met him."

"But you're not aware that Kaye Fowler and this Sellers guy knew one another?" Hearns asked.

Dr. Collier ran both hands through her hair, pulling it tight against her scalp, holding it there for a few seconds and then let it fall back down.

"They knew one another?" she asked, stunned.

"Yes, prior to the incident of Seller's death they both worked at Best Buy and it seems they dated a bit, right up to his death."

Stevens gave Dr. Collier a second to absorb the information.

"Likely scenario is that Sellers found out what Mullers did to Kaye and took matters into his own hands, probably without her knowledge, we're not sure. He was out-muscled and it ended tragically for him."

"Kaye ever mentioned any names during sessions?" Hearns asked.

Dr. Collier shook her head and her response was weak. "No, no one is required to ... actually, it's discouraged, so no, she didn't."

A few seconds passed, Stevens was about to move the interview along when she noticed Dr. Collier was about to speak.

"This is a lot to absorb right now and I'm a bit confused. How does this connect with your present investigation?"

"We also believe that after Mullers killed Sellers, Kaye retaliated by killing Mullers, we're guessing she might've been preparing for such an agenda before she met Sellers."

"Kaye killed Garrison Mullers?" asked an astounded Dr. Collier. "He was a big guy, strong, I know, and Kaye is, well, she's smaller than me and he was far too strong for me."

"First," said Stevens, "we're not saying she did it, but if she did she was clearly prepared for the task. It happens, it can be done."

"Then how does this connect her, even if she did that, to the rest of the killings?"

"Every member of this group has had their assailant killed, except the newest one," Hearns stated. "That is too much of a coincidence. Do you agree?"

"Yes, I'd have to agree," Dr. Collier answered like she preferred not to. "You think this points to Kaye having done all this?"

"Just a possibility," Hearns said.

Shaking her head. "One I find hard to believe. Seems so ... impossible."

"Carrying our suspicions further," Hearns said, "we think after she killed Mullers she joined this group, probably seeking some legit help, and after discovering the other's assailants were all out free, she felt compelled to continue."

"Like we said, this is just a possibility," Stevens added.

"So," asked Dr. Collier, "what do you want from me?"

"Nothing more," said Stevens. "You've already given us what we came for and that was to determine your level of knowledge and connection to all of this."

"And?"

"And, we know you knew very little and aren't in any way connected to the killings," Hearns stated.

"So, what do you do now?"

"We continue our investigation, and, like you, we can't divulge our plans."

"You're going to talk with Kaye again, aren't you?"

"That's likely on our list," Hearns said, rising. "Maybe you don't mention this conversation."

"No," she said, shaking her head. "I won't."

"Thanks for meeting with us again," Stevens said and rose. She shook hands with Dr. Collier and Hearn simply acknowledged his departure with a polite nod.

Dr. Collier was quiet, still in her thoughts, as she saw them out.

"Didn't know they were calling for rain today," Stevens said, turning on the wipers.

"Yeah, and tomorrow too." Hearns knew Stevens was antsy. That was why she mentioned the rain as a distraction. That meant she knew they were closing in on the final chapter of the investigation.

"Tomorrow too huh?"

"Yeah, but the weekend is suppose to be nice. You got plans?"

"You know me to ever have plans for a weekend? Or for any day for that matter."

"Fowler sound worried when you called?" he asked.

"She sounded puzzled, but not worried. She even asked me what this was about."

"Like she doesn't know."

"She asked if her husband could be there. Why do people ask that all the time, if someone can be there? It's not like they're under arrest. Just an interview."

"Just making sure, I guess. They don't know."

They pulled into the arched driveway, sat in the heavy rain in front of the Fowler's home and waited for a let-up in the rain.

Stevens craned her neck, gazed upward out of the windshield, looked at nothing but the marbling of water on the glass and the grayness of the sky. She leaned back into her seat and shifted anxiously. "Wish this would let up."

Hearns reached into the floor of the back seat, picked up the umbrella and handed it over to her.

"You take this. I'll be fine."

"We can wait a few more minutes. We're in no hurry."

He knew she was, and was about to agree when the rain let up and without discussion they both darted to the front porch canopy and found the door opening.

"What a day, huh?" asked Kaye. "I saw you pull up."

"It's a mess alright," Hearns said, brushing the moisture off his jacket.

"Don't worry about the water, it's fine. Come on in."

Kaye led them to the same room as before and it was empty.

"You're husband not joining us?" asked Stevens.

"He's upstairs on the phone with business issues. We've been so busy and are understaffed. We can't hire enough to keep up, not good people anyway."

As she spoke she directed them to their seats.

Her husband walked in. "Greg, these are detectives … I'm sorry, I forget."

Hearns, stood, leaned over and shook his hand. "I'm David Hearns and this is my partner Cathy Stevens."

Greg smiled and nodded and sat beside Cathy on the sofa.

Stevens stood and addressed Kaye. "Might work better if you join your husband."

Kaye shrugged, rose and moved to sit by Greg. "Help yourself to drinks."

Hearns sat and reached for coffee while Stevens jumped back into the topic. "We've got a few more question. Just some loose ends to clear up."

She paused, no one said anything and she continued.

"Are you aware," Stevens began, looking at Kaye, "that Garrison Mullers is the same person who assaulted Dr. Collier – Pless at the time?"

"I wasn't aware anything like that had happened to Dr. Collier." Her tone was steady and calm. "No, I had no idea."

"Were you aware that Qyntan Sellers also had connection to her?"

"No." The surprise sounded genuine. "What kind of connection?"

"He worked at Lowes, and her father was a manager there, and she said she suspected Sellers of stalking her, but she admitted she only suspected, wasn't sure."

"Then I doubt it should be said he was stalking her. Don't you think?" The tone was defensive.

"Let's move past this," Hearns said. "We suspect that Sellers was at Mullers' apartment with the intent of doing him harm, for what he knew Mullers had done to you."

"That's not likely because he didn't know Mullers was the person. We'd talked, I'd told him a few details, mostly vague stuff, about what'd happened. But I don't know how he could've know it was Mullers."

"Do you know the name Jay Blankenship?" Stevens asked.

Kaye thought for a second. "Yes, isn't that the person who abused Clark Daniels?"

"Yes, that'd be him. Do you know anything about Blankenship?"

"Just what Clark said and that's not much."

Hearns was frustrated, thinking more progress should've been made by now. "Are you aware the Blankenship was killed, murdered."

"Yes, Clark mentioned it."

"Why would he tell you?"

"I don't know, we're friends, we've had bad experiences, confided to some degree with each other. He was telling me how weird it was that the information showed up at his house and how it bothered him some that he was almost glad about his death."

Stevens was amazed how sharp Kaye was, calm, focused, and never missed a beat. That meant they were wrong about her or she's better than they expected, cooler, maybe cold. "Are you aware that every member of the group has had their assailants killed, except for the new one. Forget her name."

"Leslie Newman," Kaye said, paused in thought. "Each member of the group, the one I'm in, with Dr. Collier, they've all had the person who hurt them killed?"

"Yes, they have, and we think that's odd."

"I agree," Kaye said, sounding truly amazed. "Maybe it's more than odd, just plain freaky weird." She paused. "That's not likely a coincidence, in my opinion."

Dang, thought Stevens, she's a step ahead.

"A coincidence it's not, and we think that one person is responsible for the killings and that person had a connection to the group, maybe a member of it."

"You really think that's possible?" asked Greg.

"More than just think it," Hearns said, "we're nearly certain."

Kaye had eased back into the sofa and sat quietly in thought. "I just can't see that, not someone in the group, even if it's someone who has a connection to the group, it's not one of us." She thought for a second. "Only two men in the group would be James and Clark and there's not a snowball's chance in hell it's either of them. Of that I'm certain."

"Could be a woman," Hearns suggested. "Or someone related to, or somehow connected to them."

"I guess it could. Julie's new. Sally and Evelyn, well, just no way they could be considered. I'm the only women in the group who'd be the most able and it's not me, so this whole thing is missing the mark for me."

"You've quickly analyzed this, remarkably well," Stevens said.

"I'm sure it's the same conclusions you've considered." She looked at them both, and a smile came. "You think it could be me?"

"We're keeping our minds open," Hearns said.

"Surely you don't think …" Greg said, shaking his head, but didn't finish.

"We think a lot of things," Stevens said, as she rose. "We will until we know for sure."

Hearns was surprised the interview was ending and rose.

"Thanks for giving us your time," Stevens said.

"Sure, no problem," Kaye said. "Any time."

With Stevens and Hearns out the door, Kaye turned and gave Greg a hefty shrug. "Can you believe they think there's a connection to our group?"

Greg didn't answer.

"Well, you've got to know them like I do. We're a close group and I'd know. I'm more than one-hundred percent certain it can't be."

"They're just covering all their bases, doing what cops do," Greg added.

"I don't want to eat in tonight. Let's go out. You pick and I'll treat."

"You ready to go now?"

"Sure, if you are."

"Let me get this suit off, won't take a sec."

He trotted up the stairs while she sat on the sofa and thought about all that had just taken place. She mulled it over to pick out any potential problems.

She had to be prepared – just in case.

No words were spoken for the longest time as Hearns and Stevens drove in the late afternoon traffic. He knew she was ready to bite a nail into. He wasn't that intense, but wasn't happy.

"You still think she's a possibility?" He needed to get this rolling.

"I don't think nothing right now."

"You don't think anything right now."

"Don't start."

He smiled and thought he'd let it go, at least for now. Give her some time, that'd be the thing to do.

"I feel like I took a squirt pistol to a knife fight." She didn't elaborate.

"Maybe she's innocent."

"Maybe, maybe not. Maybe she's just prepared. Think about it. If she is the one who's doing this it's clear the person is no dummy, and never leaves a trace, nothing. Plus, if she is the one, she's physically and mentally prepared to pull off those killings. Did you see the strength in her arms and legs?"

"Well, I saw her legs right off," Hearns said with a sly smile.

"Stay focused here, this isn't the time."

"Felt like the time, at the time, guess that time has now passed."

She shook her head and a broad smile appeared. "I swear. I need a new partner."

"I know better than that, and you won't admit, but you got the best there is."

"Ha! There's nothing to admit." She knew he was right but she'd not admit it. She knew he was the best. "There's one thing we need to do before we hit her again."

"We need to interview them again, all but Clark."

"Yes, we do. Do you know why?"

"To find out if they'd been approached by anyone, like Kaye Fowler, who wanted to know the identity of their assailants."

"Exactly, Dick Tracy."

"Dick Tracy?"

"Never mind. But you're right and I bet you we'll find out that she'd lured that information out of them all."

"Lured it out," Hearns repeated. "I like that, never heard that one used. Maybe next time I get to do a news interview I'll work that one in."

"Wasting your time," she stated.

"Wasting my time, how so?"

"Trying to make yourself look smart. Wasting your time."

"Sure it's a waste of time doing what doesn't need doing."

"Dang, I'm being out-gunned by everyone today. First Fowler, now you."

"Don't take it so hard. You're still the best in my book."

"Really? You think that?"

"Yep, you got good instincts. Most would've written Fowler off. Not you. You don't back off when you smell guilt."

"You think she's guilty?"

"Doesn't matter. You think she is, I can tell, and that's all I need."

"Thanks."

"She did have nice legs."

Stevens grinned and shook her head.

Bill and Linda Bradford chatted while en route to meet with Amy Louise at the Silverdale Extended Child Care Facility. Elaine rode quietly in the back, pondered on the idea of this possible adoption and the reasoning behind it. Maybe, she can't help but think, I'm going to die and they need a … she thought replacement, but that didn't sound right. She couldn't come to a conclusion on if she liked the idea or not.

Elaine didn't know if she'd been lost in thought or if it didn't take that long to get there, but they pulled into a parking space to the side of the entrance. She glanced around and could tell it was well kept, nice play area to the far side of the building, large fenced area, plenty of good equipment. She considered if she'd not been adopted as a baby if she'd lived in a place like this. Would've been better, at least for mom and dad, me getting sick and they going through all this. It just wasn't fair, not to her, not to them. They tell her she's getting well, to keep her mind in a positive place, but she didn't feel positive and didn't feel like she was getting better. She knew many people prayed for her but it was beginning to feel like God had plans other than making her better.

No one seemed in a hurry to get out of the car.

Linda looked into the back. "You ready?" she asked Elaine.

Elaine softly nodded.

Bill stepped from the car and waited for Linda and Elaine. They entered cautiously through the front door and found the inside to be colorful and bright, clearly a place for children, There was a faint odor of fresh paint.

A lady walked past, crossing an intersecting corridor and saw them, stopped and headed in their direction. She had a warm smile, appeared to be the one who ran the place, frantic from the pace.

"I'm Raynetta," she said. "You must be Elaine?"

"Yes," she softly replied with little enthusiasm.

She held her hand to Bill, "You'd be Bill." She turned to Linda, "And you'd be Linda." She hugged her.

"Follow me," she said as if giving instruction to a child and led them into a room with shelves of book of all sorts. The library, Elaine knew. "If you'll wait here I'll get Amy Louise." In a flash she was gone.

They stood for a few second until Elaine began to walk and look around. Linda noticed a table and pointed. "Let sit while we wait."

They'd just settled and were rejoined by Raynetta, accompanied by Amy Louise.

Linda was shocked at how frail the girl appeared, not noticing the bright, intelligent eyes and radiant smile.

Bill noticed the eyes and the smile and was immediately drawn to the child.

Elaine was interested but cautious.

"This is Amy Louise." Raynetta pointed to a chair next to Linda, for Amy Louise.

Ignoring the direction, Amy Louise walked around the table and sat next to Elaine.

Raynetta smiled. "Amy Louise, this is Bill and Linda Bradford and their daughter Elaine."

"I remember their names from yesterday when you told me they were coming." Her tone was politely informative, and sweet, noticed Linda.

"How old are you Amy?" asked Linda.

"My name is not Amy, it's Amy Louise, and I'm nine." Again, she's polite and sweet.

"What do you like to do?"

"I like to play with my friends, I like to read books. This is my favorite of all the rooms. I like to eat fried catfish and German chocolate cake, and I like puppies but some dogs frighten me. I like to wear skirts and blouses and not jeans and slacks, and I like blue and red, but not green and brown, and I'll wear black if I have to go to a funeral but that's all."

Linda smiled at Bill, then back to Amy Louise. "What is your favorite book?"

"I don't have a favorite book. Some books I don't understand, but I think all books are good, unless there are some really bad ones that I've not read and then I can't say anything about that because I don't know."

Elaine thought this girl was a little odd but hadn't determined the nature of the oddness and was still undecided if this was going to be a good idea or not when Amy Louise rested her hand on her arm. Not startled, but concerned, she didn't want to be mean, or rude and didn't pull away, but looked at Amy Louise, who gazed thoughtfully at her.

"You're sick, aren't you," she stated.

Now uncomfortable, Elaine looked at her mother with curious and pleading eyes.

"Yes," said Bill, "she's been sick but she's getting better."

"Are you getting better?" Amy Louise asked Elaine, who shifted in her chair, weighed her response and suddenly felt brave.

"I don't think that I am, though people say that I am."

Bill and Linda, stunned by the words, looked to each other but said nothing.

Raynetta was not going to intervene and decide to let things play out. She knew Amy Louise.

"They only tell you that," Amy Louise said, "so that you'll not worry and make things worse for you. They don't say things like that to lie, but to be helpful. That's why they do that."

"I know," Elaine said. "But I don't feel better, but I wish I did so people wouldn't have to be sad and worry about me all the time." She shifted around towards Amy Louise. "I just want to be normal, have a regular life, go to school, grow up and get married, I want to have kids and be a good mom like my mom and marry a good man like my dad."

Linda's face flowed with tears, Bill's chin quivered, and Raynetta beamed with a smile.

"Yeah. I know what it's like to wish for hard things. I just want a nice family to be with. That's really all I've ever wanted, just that."

Linda put her opened palm over her mouth to hold back the dam that was about to burst. Bill looked into his lap and Raynetta allowed the tears to trickle slowly down.

Elaine began to cry and Amy Louise squeezed her arm slightly and asked, "You know what I've learned?"

"What?" Elaine asked.

"When I was with the last family and when I found out they didn't want me anymore I got to thinking, thinking back to the families I've been with. I learned that things were getting better each time and that soon I would find exactly what I'm looking for."

Elaine had stopped crying, tears still wet on her cheek and was enthralled with these words. "Sounds like a good thing to learn."

"Yes, it was a very good thing to learn. You know what else?

Linda, Bill and Raynetta all were aware of nothing but this small, frail child about to tell what else.

"What?"

"I think the same thing is going to happen to you. That you are going to get exactly what it is you want, all that you said is going to happen."

"Are you sure?"

"Are you sure?" Amy Louise repeated the question.

Elaine thought for a moment, smiled and hugged Amy Louise. "Yes, I'm sure."

"You've just learned something too."

The silence was loud and heavy in the room and was soon broken by Raynetta, her voice raspy with emotion. "We need to bring this lovely meeting to an end. Things to do, schedules you know."

It was on the drive home that Bill and Linda noticed the first sign of Elaine's change.

"Can we stop for a cheeseburger, shake and fries? I'm hungry."

"Of course we can," Bill said, ecstatic with joy. He couldn't remember exactly how long it'd been, but it had been a long time since she'd asked for that, which was her favorite.

Linda scooted to the middle of the seat and leaned her head on Bill's shoulder. Elaine smiled in the back seat thinking it'd been a long time since they had done that. It always made her feel good, and safe.

The drive home was completed without anyone giving significant notice to the difference between how this trip began and how it ended. But it was already in the minds of all three that there was a special, small and frail, young lady who'd soon find a new home.

CHAPTER NINE

Kaye Fowler called Carroll Grist yesterday to ask for a convenient time to drop by, stating she wanted to speak to him about something. He suspected she wanted him to take on contract work. He stood quietly, examined the Dell, and debated over his response.

He'd done contract work before and liked the money, but still had resentment from the past. They should've paid him what he was worth, paid to keep good people like him and they'd not have this issue of having to farm out work. It was probably a better deal for them, having one less regular employee to keep up with and provide with benefits. That, he knew, was the way things seemed to be heading and didn't have a strong opinion either way. She arrived as he still debated the matter, but was certain if she offered a full time position he'd decline. He'd quit to have the time and flexibility to tend to his growing needs and going back full time for them, or anyone, was out of the question. He had enough to make ends meet.

When Kaye arrived that afternoon she didn't waste time with a lot of small talk but quickly confirmed his suspicions.

"Whatever work you can take on would be helpful." She all but pleaded.

He noticed she looked different, though not sure the nature of that difference.

"My work is steady," he said and avoided eye contact, "and I'm not considering taking on anything to hinder my focus on my customers."

"Maybe for a couple of months, possibly three? It'd help me out a lot. I can boost up the money if it'll sweeten the pot for you." She smiled hopefully but was unaware of the futility of such a ploy, at least on him.

"I can do three months, but no more." This came at a good time but he'd not reveal that. That sweetening of the pot was the deal breaker for him.

"Great, Carroll. I really appreciate you doing this and we'll make it worth your time, I promise."

He nodded, and the nod slowly disappeared and he shook his head, but he said nothing.

"I'll give you a day's notice when someone will be coming to drop off work, might be a week, thereabouts, before we can get things set up."

He nodded his acknowledgement and returned to his work, ignoring her.

She shrugged and left.

She'd forgotten just how strange he was, it was like talking to a deaf/mute for the response she'd get. She knew he was as good a tech as they ever had and probably should've paid him more money while they had him. That was all history now.

Carroll Grist was quickly put out of mind as she drove to meet up with Clark Daniels. He'd called two days ago and wanted to meet with her, but didn't give any specifics. She needed desperately to go over the details of the visit from the detectives. She wasn't looking for advice or help, she just needed to talk to someone and he was the only option, even if she hadn't yet told him that his suspicions were right.

She stopped for gas and called Clark to make sure he was home, but there was no answer. She finished pumping, paid at the pump, and was buckling up when the call came. Clark said it'd be maybe thirty minutes before he was home and suggested they meet for early dinner at Marcus', to which she agreed, since it was close and convenient, though she wasn't hungry.

She parked, didn't see his car and went inside. She ordered a drink and the server had just brought her drink when Clark walked in.

"Hope this is not inconvenient," he said and slid into the booth.

"No, I was on a business errand, just got it out of the way when I called. This was closer anyway, so all is good."

"Have you ordered any food?" he asked and nodded to her drink.

"Not yet, I'm not hungry but you go ahead and eat. Won't bother me a bit."

The server stepped up, he ordered and they chitchatted until his drink was brought.

"I know you called the other day to meet up," she said, "and not sure what you needed, but something has developed since then. Those two detectives came back by, had some more questions."

Clark frowned with concern.

"They've come up with the same conclusion you did." She laughed and squirmed in her seat. "They think that all the evidence is pointing to me as the one who killed those people, you know, like Jay Blankenship and the others."

Clark leaned back in the booth. "That can't be good."

"I'm not going to mislead you any longer, Clark." She paused and considered if she should continue. "You were right, it is me."

"I've known it was, but this puts everything in a new light." He tapped his fingers on the table, his forehead furrowed. "What are you gonna do? I mean, with them suspecting you and all?"

"All they have is a theory, nothing substantial, all circumstantial and weak at that."

"But if they've come to that conclusion they'll dig more and then what?"

"I've thought about that and the only way they can narrow it further, pointing to me, is if they ask each of the members of the group if I'd approached them for information concerning their assailants."

"Did you?"

"Yes, just like I did with you, and that might end up being a big mistake. It was the easiest and quickest way to find out what I needed to know."

"Even knowing now that I was right about this, about you being the one and all, I still can't look at you and imagine you being able to pull it off." He shook his head and had a playful grin.

"Well, Mullers gave me the motivation and I trained hard. I was extremely focused. I always worked within the element of surprise. Once I get the jump on them they don't stand a chance. Truth is, outside Mullers, they were all easy."

Clark again shook his head. "Still, hard for me to imagine a little gal like you, no offense meant, doing something like that."

"Doesn't matter right now. My problem is in the right here and now, how I'm going to prepare for what's coming, or may come."

Clark didn't respond and appeared to be lost in thought.

"I have to stay cool about it and think it through," she softly said as if talking to herself.

Clark sat up straight and his eyes indicated he'd worked up his courage. "I told you I could be some help, that I could make my life count and now is the chance for me to do both of those."

He paused and calculated his words, but only said, "I take the fall for you."

"You mean take the blame for all of that?"

He nodded with a grin of satisfaction and accomplishment. "You fill me in on the details I'll need to be convincing and that will be that."

"Absolutely not," she stated. "You're not going to do that. Besides, if all is played right that'll not be necessary."

He shrugged. "Just know that's a real option right there. I'm likely dying anyway and what can they do to a dead man."

"Don't say that, Clark. You don't know you're dying and it's not good, can't be healthy to say stuff like that."

"Well, anyway, I've decided to not take those treatment. I'm looking into some sort of ... what's it called?"

"Alternative treatments?"

"Yeah, like that. But then, I'm still not a hundred percent sure."

"If you were in perfect health," she said, "I'd not let you do that. It's not an option, and besides, I think I've got all my bases covered."

He shrugged. "The offer is always there, if you change your mind."

"Won't be no changing my mind."

She picked up a frenchfry and playfully tossed it. "You're an idiot. You know that?"

He grinned. "I'm not the one caught with my thumb in the pie. You are."

"I'm far from being caught, long way from that. Even if they are one hundred percent sure in their mind I'm guilty there's not enough to take to a grand jury, not even close."

"Your masked avenger days are over then, huh?"

"I never told you I wore a mask."

"You do?" He laughed. "I had no idea."

His eyes pleaded. "Can I see it?"

"You're a doofus." She laughed, shaking her head.

They sat in silence as he finished his sandwich, picked up his drink and took a sip. He eyed her over the glass and saw both determination and worry. It popped into his mind that he wished she wasn't married. He liked her ... a lot. But he needed to push that idea way back, permanently.

"I hate to run but I've got things I have to do when I get back to work," she said. "I'll pay the tab on the way out. You leave the tip"

"Sure ... thanks," he said. "Didn't intend for you to pay."

"Business expense. Deductible."

He grinned.

She had taken only a few steps and he called out, "Hey, don't forget, the offer is always there."

She didn't turn around and waved away his suggestion. "You just focus on getting better."

She chastised herself as she drove, rolled around the idea of Clark's offer and how selfish she was. But, it was nice of him to do that. She forced the idea out of her head and it slipped back. She couldn't stop it: What if it does get desperate and Clark doesn't get better and his odds slim way down to nothing? This time it was more than chastisement, it was disgust, sick with the idea she could consider such a thing. But it was reasonable, that she had to admit. She audibly groaned at the coldness of her calculations and wondered if she was truly a sick person, maybe always had been. She had to focus, make sure the situation doesn't reach that desperate place and this craziness could be permanently put away. If she was lucky enough to slide by this she'd never attempt another killing, of that there was no doubt in her mind ... well, very little doubt.

She drove for a while, tried not to think of anything, but another thought came, that she was growing fond of Clark. He's a nice looking guy and it puzzled her that he wasn't hooked up with someone. The remembrance of his illness came and caused an ache as she thought of what might lie ahead for him.

He was a nice guy. Why did things like this happen to nice guys? It was just one more question to add to an already overwhelmed list. But Clark did understand her better than anyone. Not only better than Greg, but anyone, period. He knew the worst about her and not only cared, but wanted to sacrifice himself for her. Who, she tried hard to imagine, does that?

⊷⊶

It'd been in the back of his mind to return to Landers, though the last abduction had taken place there. He knew it would be foolish to go back so soon. Carroll Grist instead drove toward Russell, a small town in the opposite direction. He imagined as he drove how easy and convenient it would be to take someone from Markham, being a larger city, but it was too dangerous. Larger cities were easier to remain obscure and become lost in the crowd. Still, he'd not take the chance.

His mind drifted to Kaye Fowler and her recent visit. He would have extra money coming in from the work. Maybe he could do it longer than for the three months they discussed, possibly for six months. Then he thought that would look too eager and she'd renege on the boost in money and he didn't want that. He mulled over the matter and determined the offer would be presented as him being thoughtful of her predicament. That could work he concluded, and smiled at his solution.

Her change of appearance still nagged at him. If he'd unexpectedly met her on the street he wouldn't have known who she was, and it wasn't her physical appearance that'd changed. There was something about her gaze, her eyes, like a predator. He knew all about predators. But why would she have that look? He couldn't imagine what had happened to her that she had become like him.

He saw the sign, Russell six miles, then noticed the police cruiser behind him and wasn't alarmed until the lights flashed.

He pulled over, opened the glove box and pulled out his registration and proof in insurance. The officer stepped up to the window and saw him reach for his driver's license and stepped back in caution until he'd rolled down the window and handed him the items. Carroll noticed the officer had his hands near his hip, maybe his holster, but assumed it precautionary.

"You're from Markham," stated the officer while looking at the license. "You come to Russell often?"

"No, this is my first trip. Why do you ask? Is there a problem?" Carroll asked without strain, only curiosity.

"No problem, but we have a speed limit sign posted a little farther back, lots of folks don't see it and you were going a tad over the limit." The officer let that information soak in. "The reason I stopped you is your tags are expired by almost a full month."

Carroll nodded his understanding. "Okay, I remember now."

"You knew they were expired?"

"No, well, I remember getting the notice and had the intentions of taking care of it that day. Something must've distracted me because it completely left my mind … until now."

The officer smiled. "Just get that taken care of and drive careful." He returned the items, gave Carroll a small, friendly salute and returned to his cruiser.

Carroll put things back in the glove box and continued his drive. It crossed his mind he should've asked the officer about flea markets and antique shops. He pulled into a small, mom and pop grocery with gas pumps out front. Filled up, paid, returned to his car and saw the officer pull up. He hesitated and waited for the officer.

"I hope I'm not being a bother," Carroll said, "but was wondering if there are any flea markets or antique shops in town?"

"Only one I know about is straight on down the highway, just as you're leaving town. If there's more I don't know, but you can ask Helen inside, she'll know if there's one."

"Thanks, I'll do that." He returned to the store, found Helen to be the lady who'd taken his money for the gas and could tell she'd wasn't going to be a lot of help. "Was curious if there's any antique shops or flea markets in the area?

The lady acted like she was bothered by him asking, but he had that a lot and let it pass.

"Michelle's place on down the road, and this guy got a flea market type place over near the Assembly of God church, but not sure it's still up and going."

"Is that near here?"

She appeared even more bothered. "Go down," she said with a sigh and pointed from the direction he'd come, "three blocks and turn left and go down until you see the church and it's just past that, like I said, if he's still got it up and going."

"Thanks, sorry to be a bother."

"No bother," she said.

He wondered why she'd say that, since she clearly was bothered.

He looked for the place the lady had described by the church and it appeared deserted so he turned back and drove to the one the officer mentioned. The one Helen called Michelle's Place. There wasn't a sign but it was obviously the place and looked like it might have possibilities.

Only one person was inside, a lady who didn't look anything like he imagined a Michelle would. She was in her late sixties, at least, maybe early seventies and probably been smoking heavy since her teens. She looked up and gazed for only a fraction of a second and went back to whatever it was she was doing. He wasn't sure which direction to begin and veered to the right.

"You looking for anything in particular?" she asked with a deep, raspy voice, confirming his suspicion about the cigarettes.

"Old medical instruments?" he asked without expectation.

"Got some old vet stuff, about as close to medical as I might have."

"I'll just look around if you don't mind."

"Don't mind at all. Just holler if you need anything."

After a rambling tour through he decided to go, gave her a nod as she looked up.

"Nothing?" she asked.

He shook his head and stepped into the midday sun, noticed it was sunny and warming up. This was unexpected since he remembered hearing the forecast predicting cloudy and rain likely. He wished he'd asked Michelle about a good place to eat, not a fast food, possibly a diner and determined if a place like that was here it'd not be hard to find. The whole town appeared to be concentrated in about twelve blocks by maybe four.

He wasn't disappointed and soon found a diner – Darby's. It looked promising from the outside and the aroma as he stepped in immediately increased his hunger. He spotted a small table, sat down as the waitress stepped up with a menu.

"We got meat loaf, mashed potatoes, and black-eyed peas on the special. You need a menu?" She was young, fairly attractive, but wore a sheer, white blouse that was extremely translucent.

"No, the meat loaf sounds fine, thank you."

He thought it unusual to find someone dress so provocative in a place like this, in a small town. The blouse was so sheer you could see the flesh tones and the texture of her bra.

"Brown or white gravy on the potatoes?"

"Brown."

She gave him a look that indicated she knew he was looking and that it didn't bother her, as if she enjoyed the attention; even from him.

"Rolls or cornbread?"

"Rolls will do." He had no interest in the sensual attraction of the young lady. She only provided a curious distraction.

"What to drink?"

"Tea, unsweetened."

"Be right back."

He nodded as she left and thought about how perturbed his mother would be at the attire of the young waitress. He imagined his mother whispering across the table, wondering how in the world could folks dress like that, that she had to be an embarrassment to her parents. He smiled as the scene played out in his mind.

He scanned the dining room. Three tables were pulled together and packed with what appeared to be an assorted group of active and retired farmer, some handyman types, one man with a suit, had a preacher-look, and a young boy, likely in early teens. It was noisy around that table, even from where he sat on the far side of the diner.

A family of four sat nearest him, a dad and mom, two girls, one about twelve and the other close to seven or eight. The younger faced him but hadn't noticed his attentive glances.

She brought the meat loaf and sat it down, rushed off and he wasted no time devouring the lunch. As he ate he found it impossible not to watch the younger girl, until she caught one of his glances but he couldn't look away. He saw the disturbance work its way onto her face and he went back to his food and with forced effort didn't look at her again.

He stepped outside as the officer who'd stopped him earlier pulled up. He walked up to his car as the officer slid out of his cruiser.

"See you found Darby's," he said with a grin. "You ain't come to Russell if you've not eat here."

"I must agree," Carroll said. "It was delicious. Best I've had in a while."

Back in his car he debated on which directions to go and came to the conclusion it didn't matter because he felt this town was not going to produce what he was looking for. He didn't know why he knew, but he did, and almost made the choice to head back to Markham. It was summer and he expected there had to be a place in town where kids hung out, a community center, a pool, something, or somewhere.

It didn't take long and he'd found a community center with a pool in the back. The layout bothered him because adults were everywhere and lots of movement with people involved in various activities. A large crew of Hispanic men worked on mowing and trimming and the fact he'd run into the officer three times didn't help. No anonymity, no ease of egress, which would be critical, so he decided to head home.

He evidently had made a wrong turn because he was now lost and after several hopeful turns he was now at the community center again. He parked, looked around and made another attempt. He felt he'd again headed in the wrong direction, but wasn't upset or disappointed because several young children playing ahead, so he slowly drove by the children. One boy was a good choice for a pick-up. He made a complete full block turn around and drove by again. This time he stopped and rolled down a window.

There were four kids who'd been playing some mixed up game of tag or simply chasing one another. When he stopped none of the kids approached him, only stood and looked curious.

"I'm looking for a family by the name of Adamson," he said. "Do any of you know anyone named Adamson?"

"Our name is Adamson," said the tallest girl.

How coincidental he thought. "Is your father's name Thomas?"

"No."

The young boy he'd eyed moved back a few steps and appeared cautious so he looked at the boy and asked, "Do you know of anyone else named Adamson, the father's name would be Thomas?"

He'd not notice the lady who had came from behind and her voice startled him.

"Is there something I could help you with?" she sternly asked, her eyes squinted in suspicion.

"I was looking for a man by the name of Thomas Adamson."

"John is the only Adamson I know around here." She nodded in the direction of their home. "Not heard of a Thomas."

She looked at the kids. "Jason, Anna, time for lunch. The rest of you need to get in the house, it's too hot out here right now."

Carroll smiled at the lady, admired her actions and watched her gather up her two and shooed the others on. "Do what I said now. You can play later when it cools a bit."

She turned back and gave him a short reprimanding gaze and he responded with a smile.

He rolled up the window and returned to his journey home, knowing he'd not come back to Russell. Landers was becoming more inviting, yet he still couldn't determine what it was about Landers that kept drawing him back.

Amy Louise lay still in her bed and listened as whispers where exchanged in the dark by wide-awake roommates. She wasn't interested in their conversation and only thought about the Bradford family, especially Elaine. She imagined it'd not be long and they'd come get her. There was no doubt in her mind they would and never toyed with the idea they wouldn't.

What would it be like to live with such a nice family? It had to be wonderful, this she knew. She grew excited, knowing her predictions about her gradual improvements was confirmed as coming true, even faster than she expected. She tried to imagine the town where they lived. She knew it was small and that Mrs. Niles sister, who was blind, also lived there. It was probably a perfect place to be. Landers, she remembered, that was the name.

CHAPTER TEN

Stevens and Hearns re-interviewed Sally Freeman and Evelyn Brewster to determine if Kaye Fowler had contacted them for information concerning their assailants, and both stated she'd not. Stevens clearly wasn't satisfied and he could see the mix of frustration and confusion on Stevens.

"Something happened, not sure what, but something did," she said.

"Maybe they're telling the truth," Hearns said. "You know, they have no reason to lie. What could they gain?" He knew the futility of going against her hunches.

"They're covering for her, that's what it feels like to me, and I bet when we get to James it'll be the same thing as Sally and Evelyn. You wait and see if I'm not right."

"Maybe it'll be the same because they're all telling the truth." He had to play the devil's advocate, plus he wasn't sure if she was right this time.

Hearns drove and she stewed in silence for the remainder of the trip to talk with James Epperson. He'd never detected any indication from body language or speech pattern to lead him to think the ladies weren't telling the truth when asked if Kaye Fowler had approached them in an attempt to find the name of their assailants. Both said she had not and appeared as puzzled about the questions as you'd expect an innocent person to be. At the same time he knew by years of experience that Stevens was never wrong. Though it was difficult to imagine, this could be the first.

He didn't have to look at her to know the facial expression and posture. Her arms were folded across her chest, she sat upright and her expression was that of one sitting in court as the arresting officer and watching the guilty walk free. Something he knew she hated, which he did too, but her passionate dislike was a few notches higher than his, at least she was more obvious. He accepted setbacks and roadblocks to justice, most of the time, with a sort of it-is-what-it-is attitude. But she was strictly on the other side of the spectrum and didn't have it in her to allow that anyone guilty could walk free. But, and they both knew this, it happened all the time.

He pulled into James' driveway and was getting out, looked at her and she didn't seem eager to move.

"You going to sit in the car or are you going with me?" he asked.

Without responding she slowly and reluctantly made her way out of the car.

James was quick to open the door and greeted them with his usual big smile and friendly demeanor, which was even bigger and friendlier today.

They had just sat down when James stated, "Me and Margie set a date. We're getting married."

"Congratulations," Hearns said. "Looks like things are starting to brighten up for you."

Stevens wasn't in the congratulatory mood and remained quiet.

"Yeah, we'd talked about it some before. I just wanted to make sure I wasn't going to load her up with a lot of baggage from my past."

He looked at them both with his upbeat eyes. "I'll tell you the God's truth that Dr. Collier and our group really helped me get to that point. Don't know what I'd do without them."

Something warm and strong eased into Stevens mind, not understanding exactly what, but those words broke through for her.

"We're excited and glad for you, James," she said. "I know … I least I hope that the rest of your life will be wonderful."

"Thanks, both of you," he said like he'd just got approval from his parents. "I'm not sure I remember ever being this happy."

"James," Hearns said, scooting forward, "We need to ask you another question and we'll get this out of the way and be out of here."

Without losing his smile his brow furrowed and he nodded to go ahead.

"Yes," Stevens said. "We want to ask you if Kaye Fowler ever approached you in an attempt to find out the identity of your assailant."

"Why would she do that?"

Hearns shrugged. "Did she ever do that, approach you for that?"

"No, she didn't. That would be completely inappropriate, anyone doing that. Dr. Collier told us she preferred we didn't reveal that information unless we felt the need to or it worked out to be the best thing. And it never did, not for me."

He looked away in thought, then back to them. "Truth is, I can't remember anyone saying anything like that."

Oddly, Stevens was not disappointed, not now. But she'd have to give it more thought before she could determine what had happened and what had changed for her when James made that statement.

Hearns stood and Stevens followed, James remained seated as if he would like to visit a while longer but reluctantly got up.

"Again, James," Hearns said, "Congratulation in this new development. It's good news."

Stevens felt the need to hug him and did.

"Yes, James, it is good news, very good news and you deserved to finally be happy. You've been through enough."

His smile broadened and his eyes misted. "Thanks. Tell you what, when we get things set I'll give you both an invitation. Not going to be a big thing, no church or nothing like that, just a few friends."

His smile faded and he suddenly appeared uncomfortable.

"Margie, she's real outgoing and got a lot of friends, and her family lives here. Me? Well, I've sort of been a stay to myself kind of guy, you know how that goes, and I've got hardly no family around here. So if you can make it, well, it'd be nice."

"You send the invitation and we'll be there." Hearns said and Stevens nodded her agreement, did her best not to cry and hugged James again, who now looked even more uncomfortable. But his smile was still strong.

It was more than fifteen minutes after they'd left James Epperson's house before anyone said anything, and it was Hearns.

"What happened?" he asked.

"What do you mean, what happened?" Though she knew what he meant.

"There was a change in you, while we were talking with James. What happened?"

"It was something he said."

"Well, I figured as much. But what did he say that affected you like that?"

"When he spoke of how happy he was, how he couldn't remember being so happy, all I could think of was those long, miserable years, one after the other."

"And?"

"What do you mean, and? Isn't that enough?"

"It would be if you sounded like you were done."

She sighed. "What he said about the group, Dr. Collier and the members, how they helped him, and I thought even if Kaye did this, seeing the happiness, more like joy really, in James, all of a sudden it felt right and I understood."

"You understood?" He was both curious and disturbed.

"Yeah, I did. I understood why she did it. To help them, just like she did when she took out Mullers to help herself."

"You still think she did it?"

"Does it matter?"

"You know it does. It matters a lot. If she's guilty and we can prove it, it's our job to do that, to prove it."

"Is that what you want."

"What I want is for us to do our job."

"We are ... or, we have. James was the last one and they've all said the same. She didn't approach them, so that's that. We can take all we have and put it together, take it to Hazel and she'll ask if we've been in the sun too long." Hazel Yamasoto worked for the District Attorney's Office and was a close friend of Stevens.

"So, we're done?" he asked.

She looked over at him. "Unless you have an idea, yeah, we're done."

"Well, I have nothing, not right now, but I'm not done and neither are you."

Stevens said nothing, only rode and looked impassionate and directly ahead.

"If we get something, something we can go with, then you're on board with this, right?"

"Like you said, it's our job. So, yeah, sure, I'm on board."

She didn't sound on board, not at that time, but he knew once she mulled things through she'd come back around.

"My idea is to let Elaine make this decision," Bill Bradford said to his wife Linda as she thumbed through a *Southern Living* magazine. "We're for it, let's see what she says. Let her make the call."

Linda nodded and pondered quietly.

"Isn't that the whole purpose, doing this for Elaine?" he asked.

She again nodded and said nothing.

"You don't like the idea of her being the one to make the call?"

"I think you and I should be the ones," she said and placed the magazine on the end table. "We're the parents, we've got the years and experience she doesn't."

"So you think she might not want this?"

"I don't know what she wants, it just that ..." She let the sentence fade.

Bill smiled like he finally understood. "It's you who wants the child?"

She looked away. If he saw her eyes he'd know.

"I want what's good for the family and I think this will be good for the family."

"Then you think Amy Louise is the right one?"

"I do, I especially think she's the right one. It's been on my heart, a lot, and I think maybe the Lord put it there to show me the right choice."

Bill wouldn't dispute that. He respected Linda for such sensitivity.

"Least we can do is sit down as a family and let everyone express their opinions."

"Yes, we need to do that," Linda agreed. "We'll do it right after supper. How's that?"

"Works for me." He stood, grabbed his belt, shifted the buckle around straight and grinned. "What's for supper anyway?"

"Chicken fried steaks, mashed potatoes and gravy and green beans with rolls."

"Hope we don't have a lengthy family meeting else I might just doze off after a meal like that."

She laughed. "You doze off after supper regardless of the meal."

"But I generally make it thirty, maybe forty minute before I do. With that meal I might not make it fifteen." He hugged her. "I'm going to work on some paperwork in the office, got about half an hour's worth."

"Supper'll be ready about then. Stop in and holler at Elaine … about the meeting."

He nodded and left.

He stood at her door and tapped a few times, listened for her.

"Am I in there?" Elaine asked coming from behind.

Startled, Bill turned around and grinned. "Why don't you take a peek and see."

"Did you want something?"

"Yeah, mom and I wanted to have a family meeting right after supper, wanted you there."

"Sure," she said. "Is this about adopting Amy Louise?"

"Yeah, sort of, it is."

"You're not sure?"

"About what?"

"If we're going to adopt her?"

"First, I think it'd best if we take her on as a foster child. See how things will go."

"No need to do that. She belongs here. Permanently."

He considered those words a second and said, "You must be pretty sure then?"

"How can we not be sure after the visit. I thought it was a done deal that day. What's to decide?"

"Have you said that to your mom?"

"No, I just assumed …"

"Okay, then after supper we work this out and we'll just go get Amy Louise as soon as it can be arranged."

Elaine fell into him and hugged like she'd never done. He was encouraged and amazed how strong she was. "I love you, daddy."

"Well, Sister, I love you too."

Elaine laughed. "I just thought of something. You've always called me that. Sister. Now I'm going to be one for real."

He could see how happy she was and thought maybe his own happiness could give hers a good run for its money. "Well, I guess I'll have to call Amy Louise Baby Sister."

"No offense, dad," she said. "Something tells me that Amy Louise won't take to being called Baby Sister."

He chuckled. "I think we best stick with Amy Louise."

When he'd got to his office, sat down to start work but wasn't in the mood and lacked the mental focus. There were more important things on his mind. Elaine, Amy Louise and Linda, and the future they all had together. It caused him to fight the upward flow of emotion, thinking of the long road they've been on, like a roller coaster ride, with Elaine's sickness. Already he could see the improvement that he attributed to an upswing of her attitude. It wasn't over, that he knew, but he refused to think about anything but good days ahead. There was something else that kept trying to push its way into the forefront of his mind. It was about Amy Louise and what he was thinking didn't seem possible and knew it wrong to entertain such an idea. But he did know, was certain, that Amy Louise was different, not like any child he'd met, maybe no adult either. Even after he'd pushed them back, his thoughts both excited and frightened him.

The after-supper meeting wasn't needed since all was concluded by discussion during the meal. But there was one question that neither Linda nor Bill expected.

"Did you want to adopt another child just in case I died?" Elaine asked, directing the question to Linda.

Linda thought on her response, started to skirt around the issue but decided to take it head on. "No, that's not our reason, your dad and me. But, that did come to my mind a few times, but it wasn't our reason."

Linda saw Elaine needed more.

"Our reason was to bring some new life, new hope, some new blood. I felt we were drifting into a dark place, a place that'd not be healthy for anyone, especially you," she said. "I felt we needed something to spark the life back into this family and it came to me another child might do just that. At least that's the way I felt impressed."

"Is that how you felt?" Elaine asked Bill.

He scrunched up his face in concentration. "At first I didn't … I started to say I didn't care for the idea. I was concerned about adopting another child right now. We …" He thought some more. "I thought it was too much, with what you were going through."

"What you really mean," Elaine said, " is we're all were going through."

He smiled and nodded. "Yeah, I mean that. But after meeting Amy Louise there's never been another doubt in my mind.

"Nor in mine," Linda added.

"Not in mine either." Elaine looked down in thought, then up at her parents. "I have to admit that I was feeling lost and discouraged, maybe even disillusioned. I knew a lot of people prayed for me. That you did, and I did for myself, and I knew I was getting worse. I wondered if maybe God wanted me to die, at least that's what I though until I met Amy Louise. Then I knew."

"You knew?" Linda asked.

"Yeah, I knew He was answering all those prayers."

Linda looked at Bill with concern, he nodded he understood.

"Yes, sweetheart," Bill said, "He is answering all those prayers."

That night while lying in bed Linda had to say what was on her mind. "Bill, I don't want Elaine to get an unrealistic hope, especially putting that hope in Amy Louise."

"Unrealistic hope?" Bill said in question and lay quiet, thinking. "I don't think she has an unrealistic hope or putting her hope, even her faith, in Amy Louise. She said it herself, that God was answering her prayers." He was quiet again. "But you have to admit that Elaine has made a big improvement and that can't be a bad thing."

"She talks like she knows she's getting well. What if she's not?"

"Might be best for you to take the same mind as Elaine and think she's getting well. Instead of asking what if she's not, maybe ask why not. Why can't she be getting well?"

"I'm afraid if things go wrong that's she be even more disappointed, heart broken. You know?"

"If things go wrong, well, disappointment and a broken heart will be the least of her concerns, and ours."

Linda was quiet for the longest time and Bill was patient.

"We'll call Raynetta tomorrow and get the process started."

Bill rolled over, kissed her. "Good night."

"Good night," she responded as he rolled back, then lay thinking what she needed was the same confidence as Bill and Elaine, the same kind Amy Louise had. That's what she needed all along and hoped it'd soon come.

Clark Daniels stood and gazed into the fridge, knowing there was a jar of mayonnaise somewhere. The phone buzzed on the table, he shook his head and rolled his eyes. He didn't want to be bothered. He thought he knew the number, wasn't sure and answered.

It was James Epperson.

"Hope this is not a bad time," James said, detected a hint of irritation.

"Not really, was about to fix a sandwich and couldn't find ... nah, not a bad time at all. What's up?"

"Wanted to let you know, you were right, they did come by."

"The detectives?"

"Yeah, wanted to know exactly what you said, about Kaye and all."

"How did it go?"

"Went fine. They got nothing from me that could do them any good. Besides, I kinda like them, they might be coming to my wedding."

Clark softly chuckled. "Coming to your wedding? For real?"

"Yeah, but they got nothing from me on Kaye."

"Thanks, James. Hope I didn't put you in a bad position, you know, with them and all."

"Naw, not at all, I'm cool with it, anything to help one of us." He paused. "You don't reckon she did that stuff, do you?"

"Like I said, they only suspected her on account of they thought she asked us about those people, you know, who did that stuff to us."

"She did ask us."

"She was curious is all and if they knew she'd asked it'd make her look bad, you know, suspicious and everything. When I talked to her about it she wasn't worried, said it would all work out. But I felt it'd be good if we sort of helped it work out. Evelyn and Sally were cool with it too, and things went well there. So I guess all is good."

"I hope so, she's a great gal … Kaye is."

"Yeah, she is. Don't want nothing to happen, you know, not after what she's already been through. We know what that's like."

"Just glad it's done cause I was worried a bit, worried I might screw something up. But it went smooth as a baby's butt."

"Thanks again, James, and don't say nothing to Kaye about what all we did. She might not like us getting all up in this business and all."

"I'm not, don't worry about that." James paused. "Things going okay with you Clark?"

"Sure, I guess."

James heard an underlying angst, but let it go. "Okay then. I sure miss seeing you at the meetings. The other working okay for you?"

"I honestly can't get into this new group. I'm gonna ask Dr. Collier about coming back and stuff. I miss the group."

"Think you should, I mean, if the other ain't helping. We'd all like to see you come back."

"Yeah. I'll talk to her this week, the meeting's Thursday. I'm gonna get back in here and throw together something to eat. Thanks for letting me know, James. A relief knowing it went good."

"Yeah sure. You take care and if you need anything at all you just holler."

"Thanks, I'll do."

He opened the fridge door and there was the mayonnaise in plain sight, he shook his head, and gathered what he needed for the sandwich, thinking about Kaye, feeling better about things after the talk with James.

He sat alone, eating the cold sandwich and allowed his mind to enact thoughts about Kaye, careful to keep them respectful, not only because she was married, she was a nice person. He liked her and had admitted he probably liked her more than he should, accepted that nothing would, or could, ever be between them. He was afraid he'd spend the rest of his life alone, if he had much time left. He envied James having Margie, but James' good fortune didn't do him any good and he felt selfish for thinking that. He was glad for James, not that he wasn't, but he felt some good should come his way. He'd recognized the decline, he was staying inside more and going out less, not cooking and throwing together quick meals like a cold sandwich and canned soup, going to bed earlier and earlier to avoid the boredom of being alone. He knew where it was headed and also knew it would be up to him to make changes.

This he'd learned from Dr. Collier. But what he wanted more than anything was companionship.

He thought about calling Kaye to let her know what he'd done, how things had gone when the detectives interviewed James, Sally and Evelyn, how he had put that plan together. But such efforts only made things worse. Each time he was around her it stirred up the whole mess again on the inside and figured he'd best stay away from her, not talk to her, as much as possible.

He finished the sandwich, drank down the last of the tea, put things in the sink and wiped off the counter, took a shower and went to bed early.

FBI agent Belinda Swafford slid the envelope across the table where they'd gathered inside a small conference room. "The profile has been updated and we've got pictures of all the suspected victims."

Across the table sat Stevens and Hearns, Hearns reached for the envelope. "Any leads from anyone?" asked Stevens, knowing State and County also worked on it.

"Nothing, but we're stepping up the game. The last abduction was in Landers, probably no more than seventy miles from here. The closest thing we got to a lead came from there. The City Marshall there told me that a lady came in contact with an odd fellow, stranger, same day as the abduction."

"At least there's a description. That has to help," Stevens said.

"Not really," Belinda said, "seeing the lady who made the report is blind."

Hearns shook his head. "Blind? How does that add up to a lead?"

"Didn't say it did, said it was the closest thing we got. Bill, the City Marshall, said the lady was very able for being blind, able in a

139

lot of ways, had some sort of sensitivity about those things. Don't think it's anything we can depend on."

"I agree," Stevens said.

Hearns pulled the photos of the abducted children, looked it over several times. "Take a look at this." He passed the photos to Stevens.

She held it and quietly scanned through them. "That's not hard to spot. All are about the same age, I'm guessing between six and nine, all white kids, mostly girls, with light hair and eyes. Appears the guy has a particular agenda, or motive, not sure which, maybe both. But definitely taking them for personal reasons."

"Yeah," Belinda agreed. "Only two likely reasons anyone would be abducting kids would be for personal appetites or for trafficking, and if it was trafficking it'd not be isolated to just one type like we see in the photos."

"Which only makes it more difficult," Hearns said. "You still think the guy is from around here?"

"Probably, and if not in the city, on the edges. All seems to hub from here. My guess is the guy is trying to stay away from home and in doing so that points to home. I think the guy is smart, so not sure how he missed that. There's a list of all the sex crime offenders from this area." She nodded to the envelope. "We might give them some attention but I don't think he'll be one of them. This one isn't like that."

"I agree," Stevens said, emptying all the contents of the envelope. "This one is shaping up odd."

"Yeah, that he is," said Belinda. "What's the progress on the serial killing case?"

"Dead end right now," Hearns said.

"All we've got is a long shot suspect and nothing firm there," Stevens added.

"We really need to put more time into this," Belinda urged. "It's not going to stop until we stop it. I got that feeling."

Hearns sighed. "Not much to go on."

"I know and that's why we need to put out more effort. We need a break and we need it yesterday. That's what my boss told me."

"We'll go over things with Captain Reynolds," Hearns said. "Then we'll know where we can put our efforts.

"I've talked with him and he said outside the serial killing case this would be next on the list."

"Then we need to catch him up on that," Stevens said, "and we'll see what he says."

Hearns felt Stevens was eager to drop that case. Too eager and he suspected why, but wasn't sure if he wasn't about to relent himself. Right or wrong, it did seem to have gone cold and when it came to finding someone who killed … He realized the direction his thoughts were taking and stopped them.

It was late that afternoon before they were able to see Captain Reynolds and he wasn't ready to let go of finding the serial killer.

"You work on this child abduction, I'll get someone on this serial killing, maybe fresh blood is what's needed."

Stevens didn't like it, but was careful to not show it, made eye contact with Reynolds and nodded her acceptance.

Hearns didn't like it, but for a different reason. He didn't want anyone to solve what appeared they couldn't. But he too nodded his acceptance.

CHAPTER ELEVEN

Camille Cooper watched the report of the abductions, recalled the experience of the strange man in the neighborhood and debated what to do. Her husband Charlie often told her she was paranoid and an overly protective mom and decided if she did call Jess she'd not tell Charlie. Then maybe she was over reacting, or acting more by how odd the man looked than the actual circumstance. Maybe the guy was harmless and a person couldn't help the way they looked. But her rule was to err on the side of caution so she contacted Russell Police, made up of Jess Woods and Pat Parkinson, with her suspicions. Woods called the number provided, and was put in touch with Belinda Swafford, drove to Markham to meet with her.

That she was too tiny and cute to be an FBI agent was Woods' first impression of Belinda and felt funny maintaining his professional composure. It was like he was speaking with young girl.

"I felt this was something you need to know about, call it a gut thing."

"Definitely, you have no idea how desperate we are for the least little clue." She only prayed this would be that one thing to set the progression in motion.

"We don't have anyone who can draw up a sketch, but not only did Mrs. Cooper see this man but so did I, plus I have a tag number on the guy."

She felt her heart leap with anticipation.

"Trouble is," he continued, "I run the number and the plates don't match the vehicle he was driving. Fact is they don't match anything. It's like he made them up himself, I don't know, it's odd. I even looked at his driver's license and have racked my brain but for the life of me can't remember the name, only that he was from Markham."

Though disappointed she wasn't about to lose sight of the good fortune of the description. Plus the fact the plates didn't match the vehicle was a red flag, and knowing she had been right about his location. "I'll get someone who can work with you to get a sketch drawn up, then you can run that by … I forgot her name, the lady who reported it, and see if she feels it's a good one."

Woods nodded. "I'll do what I can and spend whatever time needed to catch this guy." He looked down and shook his head. "I seen him three times that day, pulled him over when I seen his tags were expired, and I was having problems with my computer, plus it didn't seem a need at the time. Wasn't until later that I did."

"Don't kick yourself, you did nothing wrong. Just routine stuff, it happens all the time."

Woods nodded, still bothered knowing the guy was out there and might take another child and he could've stopped it.

He waited an hour and a half and worked three more hours with the artist until they had a sketch. He'd only done this two other times and never felt the sketch was good enough. He didn't know what else to say to improve this one. What the sketch could not relay, thought Woods, was the man's eyes. You can't draw something like that, something you have to see first hand.

"We'll have this aired out tomorrow, after I hear from you," Belinda said as Woods prepared to leave. "Thanks for this." She held up the paperwork. "This is like a gold mine right now. We've had nothing until this."

"Yeah, I sort of know how that goes, though we don't get many big cases in Russell, not like this anyway." He opened the door, looked back. "You need me for anything just give me a holler. Anything."

She nodded and smiled her appreciation. "I'll do that."

Belinda knew how the guy felt. She'd felt the same way at times. She also knew that it took lots of missteps to get to the right end, and now it seemed they could be headed that way. She also knew Stevens and Hearns would be anxious to know the news, called and could hear her sigh with joy over the phone.

⊨⊰⊱⊨

Amy Louise sat in a tall, straight-back wooden chair, anxiously swung her legs and waited for the Bill, Linda and Elaine to arrive. It'd taken a little longer than she expected but never doubted the outcome. She looked at the clock every ten minutes and Mrs. Niles had told her that it'd likely to be close to noon when they arrived, yet she insisted on sitting, luggage neatly arranged beside the chair.

Raynetta often peeked around the corner and each time shook her head and smiled to herself, knowing this time Amy Louise would not be coming back. That's not what made her smile, it was that she'd finally found her home, not just a home, and not for a while but for good. Plus, with Amy Louise in Landers she'd be able to regularly visit her when she visited Lavetta.

Amy Louise heard the knob of the door turn and quickly slipped off the chair, absentmindedly brushed off her skirt and took a deep breath. It was the FED-Ex man, who smiled and nodded as he walked to the counter, set the package down and waited. Mrs. Niles soon appeared, signed and the man left. She looked at Amy Louise, tilted her head to the side and gave her a wink. "They're coming."

"Oh, I know." That was all she said and slipped back into the hard bottom chair, straightened her skirt and placed her glasses even on the bridge of her nose.

"Are you hungry?"

"No, I'm not, not right now I'm not. I expect we'll stop on the way home and eat. Don't you expect that we will?" Her delight in saying 'on the way home' was evident.

"I expect so," said Raynetta, mixed with sadness and encouragement. She didn't doubt the dependability of the Bradfords but knew if let down this time it'd be painfully different. She hesitated, debated if she should go back or stay with Amy Louise until the Bradfords arrived but the decision was made for her when they stepped through the door as Amy Louise hastily slid off the chair, stumbled two steps forward, straightened her glasses and stood erect with expectation.

There was no further hesitation or time for uncomfortable silence as Elaine made several long and quick steps and embraced Amy Louise.

"I'm so glad to see you again." She released the embraced, placed her hands on Amy Louise's shoulders and leaned back, looked her in the eyes and asked, "You ready to go home?"

"I've been ready for a long time."

Linda knelt and hugged her. "So you've been up and ready early today?"

"Yes, I have. But I've been ready to go home for a lot longer than today."

Bill stood by and watched with a big smile and nodded to the luggage. "Is this all?" he asked Raynetta.

"Yep, that's the lump sum of it right there."

"If it's okay," Bill said, "I'm going to start carrying it out to the car."

"You've got our permission," Raynetta said. "I'll help if you need it."

"No, I've got it." He grabbed two of the three pieces and left, returned and picked up the last one, the largest. "Let's hit the road," he said. "If it's okay with Amy Louise we're going to stop on the way home and have a nice celebration dinner."

Amy Louise looked and smiled at Raynetta who smiled and winked, then hugged her. "You take care of these folks. They seem like good people."

"I will." Amy Louise took a deep breath and exhaled slowly and out came relief, sadness, joy and years of denied hope. "Thank you for being so helpful and nice."

"Well, you're very welcome my dear. And don't be going and thinking you'll not be seeing me. I'll be visiting off and on when I go see my sister."

"Yes, your sister who is blind."

"Yes, that sister. Lavetta."

"It will be nice when I get to meet her."

"She's mean and cranky, so don't get too excited about it."

Amy Louise smiled. "She's not mean and cranky."

"Well, don't say you've not been warned." And she hugged her again. "You best get going." She gave her a playful swat on the behind. "You've got a celebration dinner to attend."

"I do." She looked at Elaine, who still held her by the hand.

"You ready, Sis?" asked Elaine.

"I'm ready." And they headed out with Bill behind them. Linda stepped up to Raynetta and hugged her. "Thanks for everything and anytime you want to stop by, you come on, just call to make sure we're home."

"Oh, don't worry, I will." She watched Linda as she pulled the door shut and became instantly aware of something and thought of its significance: Amy Louise had never allowed anyone to call her anything but Amy Louise, at least not without politely correcting them. She'd heard her do it countless time, without fail, but when Elaine called her Sis, she accepted it completely. She could tell this was a new beginning for Amy Louise, and a good one.

Alton Duncan paced around the large room, his hands fidgeted as he fumed and thought of the insolent manner of those who knew nothing of what they spoke and how easily they offered their uninformed opinions. A fool, he considered, is known by their many words and still say nothing of value. Klaus Braxton was a perfect example of such a fool. Why would anyone question thousand of years of established traditions as old as civilized man, passed through generation after generation with no need of amendments, of alterations? One man who thought he could interject change – when he was still able to think. It'd happened before and once such attitudes arose, next to follow would be vocalization of their dissatisfaction for the larger audiences, and that would not be allowed, was never tolerated. No price or sacrifice was too great to protect the inner circles of Cain's Vineyard and the sacred mission of the nineteen sixty, one thousand, nine hundred and sixty men whose souls were etched with the commission of a divine duty. There had been other fools that had to go away and their footprints forever vanished, not to be remembered.

It was because Klaus had been a close friend. This was why he was so disturbed, why he paced and fumed, it wasn't his habit, this he knew. But to allow the induction of women was sheer lunacy, and it wasn't a sexist position and never was, though it'd not matter what it was labeled. It was simply an obviously practical matter that didn't take great intelligence to understand. Women and men were not the same, a well-understood truth no educated mind argued otherwise. But, Klaus persisted. It wasn't a matter of superiority versus inferiority, only a matter of design and propensity. Women, with their maternal inclinations, or whatever that could be properly called, could not handle the practice of molchomorism, the sacrifice of lambs, the premier rite of Cain's Vineyard, one that must be guarded with dire vigilance, a duty Alton took more serious than his own life, being one of the seventy, an elder and a priest.

It was after The Flood, when Amri found the stored tablets, meticulously etched granite, the reformation that become known as Cain's Vineyard, to be later hindered during the Great Confusion, reestablished to continue to the present, to bring mankind into the last progression, the eighth realm.

The removal of Klaus took care of a primary problem, but Alton suspected there was another in development, though not confirmed. He'd seen the reports of the abducted children, the efforts to locate the guilty party and he would reinforce vigilance to make sure they remained insulated, if this was indeed one of their sources. Edward Ross had shared his concern and this only served to heighten Alton's. He'd trace it down, determine if it was a source and if a scapegoat would be needed and a good cover provided. It was possible it'd need to be permanently shut down, though he hated to lose any source, being hard to establish. There were presently nine children in their local chambers, which put the total at twenty-three, almost a two year supply, so it wasn't urgent, providing enough time to establish new sources if required. Larry Davis would be the right person to track it down, being outside the circle, dependable and expendable.

Davis began the investigation the next day, told only what he needed to know to do the job and never asked questions. Never do less or more than instructed. He was two levels from being initiated and wasn't about to mess it up, not now, not after all he'd been through.

Alton remembered when Davis was recruited through a local civic organization, one of the many pools of potentials, trained step-by-step, unaware that he was now in a precarious place, in the isolation zone, where his suspicion-free elimination could be swiftly executed. If he proved a good servant he'd be instructed and prepped for initiation, all of which he knew nothing, only his present task. His kind never made it beyond a few levels past initiation, serving as logistical drones in highly sensitive matters, and assassinations when needed. Even among the nineteen sixty were those capable of going rogue, though extremely rare.

Secrecy was too mild a word for Cain's Vineyard's methods of operation, hidden beneath layers and behind facets of misdirection, where questions and probing lead to one conspiracy theory after another and all in the wrong direction. In a world that clamored after Elvis and UFO sightings it was easy. Still, extreme caution always was the rule, for not everyone were fools.

Now that Davis was on the job he hoped to focus on his next project: Selecting the next sacrifice.

Making his way to the chamber, where there were no need for a guard, not with the mechanisms in place, he passed through the first passage, down the short L-shaped hallway, through the second passage and faced the third and final. He placed his hand on the pad, stared into the screen and waited. He heard the hum and opened the door, placed the key into the lock and turned and entered the living quarters of the lambs. Of the nine children, seven girls and two boys, one of the boys showed resentment and hostility. Because of his negative influences he had been selected for removal, though they were usually selected according to their time in the chambers. Those who'd been there the longest had dead and lifeless eyes. The newer ones had some spark left. This boy was too aggressive and removing him would be the best move.

"You come with me," he said to the boy who showed no fear, only mild curiosity.

"Where am I going?" the boy asked, the aggression that had brought this selection upon him still evident in his voice.

"You're being moved – that's all you need to know."

"Am I going home?"

"You only need to know that you're being move." Alton beckoned the boy, who stood without showing signs of moving.

"You're going to resist?"

The boy wouldn't answer.

"I'd think you'd be glad to be able to move up, to leave this place," Alton said in a low voice. "Surely it must be boring here."

"Where am I going?"

Alton stepped closer, leaned in and whispered. "I can't discuss this in front of the others."

The boy nodded he understood and showed what might have been a faint smile. As Alton led the way the boy followed through a door other than the one from which Alton had entered, and down a hallway. The boy waited while the next door was opened and Alton allowed him through first. The room was furnished with entertainment devices and a large well stocked fridge, a huge viewing screen covered a large portion of one wall.

The boy looked at Alton with anticipation and question.

"This is temporary, you'll be here a few days." He smiled. "A big improvement, huh?"

The boy nodded but didn't smile or say anything, suspicious by nature.

"The fridge has food and drinks and a microwave for cooking. I'm afraid you'll have to make do with what is."

And Alton left without more instructions.

The boy was hesitant to move, understood that something was not right, but didn't know what was wrong.

Three days later the only mercy he'd be shown is a mild sedative, more for the convenience of those who preformed the ritual.

Darkness was setting in when the Bradfords returned, Amy Louise now an official unofficial part of the family, since the actual adoptions would be months in the future. No one was tired as the excitement of the event still maintained its high. Bill carried in the largest and medium of the luggage and Elaine carried the smallest, with Amy Louise on her heels.

"Hope you like your room," Linda said to Amy Louise as they walked in.

"It's very nice, thank you." She gazed around, but appeared subdued.

"Something wrong?"

"I get a room of my own?"

"Yes," Linda said and remembered she was accustomed to sleeping with others in the room. "Are you afraid to sleep alone?"

"No, I've done it before." She hopped up backwards and sat on the edge of the bed. "It's a very nice room, thank you," she said with forced enthusiasm.

"If it's okay," Elaine said, "maybe she can move into my room and sleep there." She looked to Linda who looked to Bill.

"Works for me," Bill said.

"I've no problem with it," Linda added.

"Can she sleep there tonight?" asked Elaine.

The hopeful look on Amy Louise's face was almost comical. Linda laughed and shook her head. "Sure."

"I'll start taking the bed down," Bill said.

"She can sleep in the bed with me tonight," Elaine said. "We can move the bed tomorrow, or some other time."

Bill shrugged. "It's a full size. That enough room for you two?"

"Sure. I barely weigh a hundred pounds and I doubt Amy Louise is even close to that."

"Eighty nine," she stated. "I weigh eighty nine pounds."

"See? Plenty of room."

"You okay with that?" Linda asked Amy Louise.

"I am." She beamed.

"Leave the bags in here," Linda said to Bill as he began to lift one. "At least for now."

He sat the luggage down. "I've got to take care of some things in the office. May take a while, so if I miss bedtime, have a good night sleep. Both of you."

"I'll leave the two of you alone." Linda squatted down to Amy Louise and hugged her. "Good to have you here, Sweetheart."

"Good to be here ... May I call you Mom?"

"You most certainly can. That would be nice. Let me know if you need anything."

"Let me show you my room," Elaine said as she hurried away with Amy Louise having to almost trot to keep up.

Standing just inside the room, Amy Louise looked around with awe. It was a perfect room, just like the room she'd imagined in her mind, even before she'd met Elaine.

"You like it?"

"I do. I like it very much. It's like my dream."

"Your dream?"

"Yes, I've dreamed of this room. This very room."

"You've dreamed of this room? My room?"

"I have."

"Not a room that's like my room, but this room?"

"Yes, it's the same. Everything's the same."

"Was I in the room when you dreamed about it?"

"I can't remember."

There were several seconds of silence.

"I'm tired. I'm going to dress for bed." Elaine was eager to change the subject.

"I'll get my clothes for bed from the luggage," Amy Louise said. "I'll dress there and be back."

Fifteen minutes later she returned and looked as prim and proper for bed as she did in her blouses and skirts.

"Which side do you want?" Elaine asked.

"I'd prefer the left side, I tend to sleep on my right side. That way I'll not breath morning breath on you when I wake up. Karen used to breath morning breath on me, that's how I know about morning breath."

"Then you sleep on the left side and it won't matter if I have morning breath since you'll be facing away."

"Exactly." Amy Louise looked concerned. "I'm not being any trouble am I?"

Elaine hugged her and practically lifted her from the floor. "You'll have to try a lot harder than that if you're trying to be trouble.

Amy Louise giggled softly, the first time Elaine had heard her come close to laughing and committed to the goal of getting a full blown laugh from her before next weekend.

Later, the lights out, both in bed, Amy had a question. "Did it bother you that I didn't see you in the room, in my dream?"

"Why do you ask?

"I could tell, at least I think I could tell."

Elaine didn't answer.

"Just because I didn't see you in the room, or can't remember it, doesn't mean you're going to die and not be here."

"How did you know that was what I was thinking?"

"I wasn't sure, I just thought about it."

"So I'm not?"

"I thought you knew you're not." Amy Louise paused in silence in the dark room. "You'll become a grandmother, you wait and see. Not soon, but you will."

"I hope not soon." Elaine laughed and leaned over and kissed Amy Louise on the cheek. "Good night."

"Good night."

Amy Louise lay breathing slowly and softly, and soon was listening to Elaine's steady breathing, thinking how wonderful it was at that very moment. She knew this was home, her home and her family. She knew this for more reasons than just wishful thinking. She knew she was where she belonged, not just for her own benefit, but for other reasons as well, and it was only recently she'd become aware of the development of something bigger than she'd thought of before.

She often wondered why she couldn't remember having a mother, or a father. But she didn't, and only assumed it was because she was too young when she first came to be with Mrs. Niles, who was the closest thing to a mother she'd had, until now.

Carroll Grist didn't like it, though it was more an inconvenience than a real problem. With the broadcast description, even though he thought it didn't look that much like him, he'd still need to make adaptations. A cap and lightly shaded glasses would be enough; it didn't take much to make a difference. He'd thought a wig would help, but that seemed too theatrical and unnecessary – the cap and glasses would do.

As a precaution he'd make a new set of plates for the car, easily and quickly done. He should be ready by next weekend for a trip. It'd have to be Landers since he's still drawn to that place.

He pondered on why he felt so compelled to return to Landers, considered it was either an omen of good or bad and smiled at the obviousness of his conclusion. It didn't feel ominous in nature, it felt good and maybe all was leading to that one special child. He hoped it was because he was beginning to question his lack of success in all his efforts. He was still the same today as he was five, even ten years ago; nothing had changed. And what specifically has he hoped for, what changes did he desire that couldn't be confronted and he make himself? He doubted anything outside extensive cosmetic surgery could help his appearance and everything else was a matter of becoming active instead of passive. He could start getting out more, interact with people, something he'd done less since leaving Computer Power.

He pushed the issue out of his mind, committed to the trip next weekend to Landers. He at least had to make this trip. The urge that compelled him was strong. Maybe this would answer everything, and maybe all was leading to this one end. He couldn't quit now, not this close to the possibility this was the moment for which he'd hoped.

The phone disrupted his thoughts.

"Yes?" he answered.

"Carroll, this is Kaye. I wanted to let you know that a man will be dropping off two pieces tomorrow morning. You still good with that?"

He wanted to say no. "Yes, that's fine."

"All information is on the work form, one for each." She paused. "You sure this is going to work, you sound unsure."

"I had something on my mind when you called and took me a moment."

"Oh, okay, I'll be in touched. If you have any questions, give me a call." She paused and waited for a response. "Thanks again, Carroll."

He didn't respond and ended the call.

Kaye looked at her phone, shook her head and thought he was as odd on the phone as he was in person.

CHAPTER TWELVE

"It's a waste of time." Hearns expressed his opinion about making another visit to Kaye Fowler.

"I know that," Stevens confessed. "But we've got to talk with her one more time, at least I do."

"It's not ours anymore. Besides, what do you expect to find out?" Hearns asked.

"I'm not sure we'll find out anything, and I may not be making this last visit as a cop, maybe it's a personal call."

Hearns pondered on how to respond. "Maybe you should explain what you mean by that."

"I'm not sure. All I know is I need to make one more call and I'll play it as it happens, things will fall where they will."

He shrugged. "I can go along with that, but I'm worried about you saying it's personal. If we go, we go as cops and nothing more."

She shrugged. "It's all the same to me."

He nodded. "Yeah, I guess you're right. Then we set it up and see how it goes."

"It's set up." She glanced at the dash. "In one hour."

He smiled. "When were you going to tell me?"

"I just did."

They stopped for lunch, lingered at the table until time and headed to meet with Kaye Fowler.

Each time they pulled up to the Fowler home Stevens couldn't help but wonder how a person could jeopardize a nice lifestyle by becoming a self-appointed avenger, if she was. But, every avenger was a self-appointed vigilante. Maybe long ago someone said something has to be done about all this craziness and maybe that someone decided they'd be the one to take care of it.

She never liked it when her thoughts took that direction.

Kaye opened the door with what appeared to be a genuine smile, warm and easy, wearing shorts and a T-shirt; the first time Stevens was able to see the hard tone of her body and only fueled her suspicions.

"Sorry for the casual dress," she said. "Didn't think you'd mind."

Hearns considered it a nice move, if she was guilty, and if not, an insignificant issue.

Stevens was glad to see Greg would be sitting in. What she hoped to say would move along easier with him present. She ignored the coffee, Hearns poured a cup and she jumped into the matter at hand.

"We stopped by to let you know we're going to be off the investigation of the killer of Jay Blankenship and the others. We've been reassigned to another."

"That's why you stopped by?" Kaye asked with suspicion. "To tell me that."

"Not really," she said. "But I'll get to that. We've passed along the reports of all interviews to the new detectives, so they may or may not be back around. Doubt they'll start from square one."

"Why were you taken off?" Greg asked.

"We considered the case at a stand still and another case was developing, one we had personal connections to and interest in."

157

"If you considered it at a stand still, the case, why reassign it?" Kaye asked.

"Our boss wasn't satisfied it was ready to be shelved," Hearns said.

Kaye nodded her understanding. "Then why are you here?"

"I needed personal closure," Stevens said. "So this visit is more personal than business."

"You think it wise to tell me that?" Kaye asked.

"Why do you ask?" Hearns questioned.

"I don't know, the tone is not that of a friendly chat and I detected suspicion." She looked to Stevens. "Even some accusation."

Stevens scooted forward and hunched over, eyed Kaye firmly, but not hard. "I'm going to be honest with you. I think you're the one who did those killing."

"I know you do," she calmly said. "I just don't know what else I can say to convince you otherwise. None of the evidence says I did it, so why keep focusing on me."

Stevens shrugged. "Let's just say it's my gut feeling. That's it."

"I'm going to assume it's not personal," Kaye said with a smile.

Stevens smiled back before she could stop it. "No, it's not personal.

"Looks to me," Greg said, "it'd be a worthless effort, considering the type of people that were killed, to continue wasting money and time on this. I mean, I know it's never a good thing to take matters in hand like that."

Before Stevens or Hearns could answer, Kaye said to him, "The law is the law. That's the way it works. It's their job."

Hearns had things to say, but felt them moot at this point. Stevens found no satisfaction in Kaye answering for them, but she was right. Hearns stood, anxious to leave. Stevens slowly rose and joined him, fighting the urge to say more but not knowing what.

Hearns and Stevens had just left and Kaye closed the door, turned to see Greg staring at her. "What's wrong?"

"I don't know, but something occurred to me, something very convincing."

"What?" she asked.

"That you did those things, that you are guilty." There wasn't a tone of accusation, only of realization.

There wasn't an expression to indicate her surprise, denial or admission. "How can you say that?"

"I don't know," he admitted. "Maybe her gut feeling rubbed off on me, and suddenly, as odd as it sounds, it made sense."

"Made sense?"

"Yeah, it's why you were trying to end our marriage, the issue you were dealing with, the uncertainty of how things would go. It made sense."

She hoped she wasn't showing her surprise, that he could put all this together based on so little and at the same time be right. She shook her head and grinned. "You should've been a cop." She walked away.

He realized she'd not admitted or denied. "Look, if you did or you didn't, I want you to know that I love you and all this is history and to be forgotten."

She turned, looked at him in amazement, walked back and hugged him. "Oh Greg, I'm sorry for all that. I was just mixed up then, that's all."

He put his arms around her. "I love you, Kaye. I couldn't bear it if I lost you, for whatever reason."

In her mind, it sounded without conviction or passion, as if said because it was expected, or like he was playing a role.

"I love you too, and thank you for being so patient."

Kaye felt guilty, but not for the reasons the detectives stated. She felt guilty because should be totally committed to Greg – but was thinking of Clark Daniels.

⚜

"So, you satisfied?" Hearns asked as they drove away.

"It doesn't matter," she said. "It's time to move on and focus on this new thing."

"Well, no big doors are opening there either." He hit the brakes hard. "Did you see that idiot?" A pickup had run a stop sign.

"You gonna chase him down?" she asked and grinned.

He shook his head. "The idiot. People could get hurt."

"People make mistakes, he ran a stop sign, probably didn't know he did it."

"I doesn't matter, it's dangerous."

She laughed. "That's a revelation. You must've graduated at the top of your class at the academy, putting together that piece of police work."

"Probably talking on the phone, or worse, texting," he said, still fuming and shaking his head in disgust. "Idiots."

"So what we got on this child abductor?" she asked. "He lives in this area, apparently tall, odd facial features and has serious demeanor."

"Don't say it."

"Say what?"

"You know."

She laughed when she caught on but said nothing and sat smiling.

"I've not got odd facial features," he stated.

"Depends on what one would call odd."

He scooted back into the seat, sat up taller. She knew he was irritated.

"Look at Jack Nicholson," she said. "He has odd facial features and he's considered a handsome man, by some."

"I don't look like Jack Nicholson."

"I didn't say you did, only stating that a person can have odd facial features and not be ugly, even considered handsome. I saw on a TV program once that Uma Thurman's facial makeup is not within the mathematical parameters for what is considered attractive. But, look at her."

"You think I'm a fairly handsome man?"

"Sure I do. In an odd, nonmathematical way, and you look more like Uma than Jack."

He laughed and shook his head. "Well, we still haven't much to go on. Dead end on one case and nothing to dig into on the new one."

"Exactly." She folded her arms, sat erect and sighed.

He felt the same way.

"Did she tell you how mean I was?" Lavetta asked Amy Louise.

Linda, Elaine and Amy Louise were out shopping, saw her sitting on one of favorite benches and stopped to visit.

"She did, and she said you were also cranky."

"Did she? Well I'll be, she must've only recently added that one. She used to only say I was mean." She shook her head and laughed. "Looks like I'm also cranky now."

"But I knew she was joking, and I told her I thought so."

"But what if she'd not joking?"

"She is, I can tell. You're not mean and cranky?"

Lavetta smiled. "How can you tell?"

"Your dog."

"Lucy? Did Lucy tell you I wasn't mean and cranky?"

"She did."

"And you'll take the word of a dog?"

"They don't lie."

Lavetta laughed heartier. "You're right there. They don't." She leaned forward. "Why don't you give me a hug."

Amy Louise hugged her a long time.

"Now that, my dear, is what I call a hug. You got a gift for that."

Amy Louise released the hug but still held to Lavetta's right hand. "I'm sorry you're blind."

Linda glanced uncomfortably between Amy Louise and Lavetta, but Elaine smiled and waited.

"Well, once a time long ago I was sorry too, but no more. You have to get over being sorry and learn to do with what is, not what you wish to be."

"You do that very well. I wish it could be that you could see again. But it can't."

Lavetta pondered the peculiarity of those words. "No, don't reckon it can." She frowned and looked down at her hand, the one held by Amy Louise. "You got something there, don't you?"

Amy Louise released her hand, looked away, then back. "I'm glad we got to meet. I told Mrs. Niles that I wanted to meet you and now I have. And I'm glad I got to meet Lucy. She's very nice."

"Not mean and cranky like some folks we've heard about." Lavetta smiled.

"Yes, not like that." Amy sat on the bench beside Lavetta. "You're like Mrs. Niles, but you only a little bit look like her. But you are very kind like her. She was the nicest person I'd ever known. Now I know several very nice people."

"Lucky we are too, to have such people in our life," Lavetta said.

"Yes," Elaine said. "We are."

"Amen to that," Linda added.

"May I stay and sit with Miss Lavetta while you go to the store?"

Linda appeared concerned, thought a second. "Sure, but stay here with her. Don't wander off."

"I won't wander off. I promise, I'll sit right here and not go anywhere."

"I'll look after her," Lavetta stated. "She'll be fine. Now go."

Linda and Elaine returned to the car and Linda looked over at them sitting on the bench like two old friends chatting away. Lucy's tag wagged as she watched them with interest. It was the same when they returned, the two engrossed in an apparently captivating discussion

"You ready to go?" Linda asked as she and Elaine stepped up.

"Yes," she answered, stretched up and kissed Lavetta on the cheek, slid off the bench and took Elaine's outstretched hand.

"We've got us a very special new friend here," Lavetta said to Linda, the tone was weighty, suggestive.

"She's special alright and we love her to death," Linda said with obvious joy.

It was clear to Lavetta as she watched them return to the car that Linda had not discovered all there was to know about Amy Louise, but Elaine's understanding was profound and beneficial, and imagined it'd be soon and Linda would come around.

Shoot, she thought, even Lucy knew it.

⇒╪ ╪⇐

Carroll Grist wasn't fond of driving in rain that blew as hard as this, and would've canceled this trip to Landers if the weather channel hadn't stated the rain would be clearing out early. He didn't mind a slow steady rain and liked the stability of his Subaru in bad weather, handling well on snow, though they didn't get much snow and nothing was safe on ice, in his opinion. The upside was the cloudy weather removed the glare of the sun and its early morning flickering through the random picketing of straight pine on that particular stretch of highway.

He considered possibly finding a place to stop, concerned that he couldn't see that far ahead, when he noticed it was beginning to ease up and the sky slowly brightened and he relaxed. He recalled his dad laughing at his mother who was extremely anxious when riding during a heavy rain. But he considered it a sensible concern as it proved often to cause many accidents, some fatal.

He'd not yet entered the city limits of Landers and noticed a large café on the left of the highway, one he'd missed his last trip, and slowed, then stopped for approaching traffic and crossed over. He noticed two semis of the same logos pulled side by side, but he didn't need those to confirm his knowledge this was a good place to eat. It was ten forty-five AM and the lot was nearly full.

He stepped inside, looked around the dining room to see it was full until he saw the small table near the hallway that had the sign pointing to the bathrooms. He chose to pass on that one. He didn't like its proximity to the high traffic walking by. He decided to wait for a table to open up and looked for a place to stand out of the way when a couple, man and woman, rose to leave. He waited until they'd stepped away and took a seat as an elderly man, who could be mentally disabled to some degree, judged by his mannerisms, began to clear the table.

Carroll noticed the man wouldn't make eye contact and focused wholly on his duties, which he performed swiftly and quietly. Maybe he's not mentally disabled, only socially awkward, and realized he was debating with himself on an insignificant matter that his mother would often make an issue, wondering this and that about people, scrutinizing everyone. This time the memory didn't bring a smile, but pity, and maybe it was pity for the old man and he forced the subject out of his thoughts as the waitress walked up.

"What'll you have?" she asked and he noticed she blinked often, like a tic.

"What's the special today?"

"Fried chicken, mashed potatoes, green beans and corn. The green beans and corns are mixed together."

"I'll have that, with unsweetened tea."

"Rolls be okay, we don't have cornbread today."

"Yes, rolls are fine."

He slowly sipped the tea and found the noise annoying, as if each one was trying to talk over another and the volume only escalated, and brief periods when it'd ease down, then right back. He quickly finished the meal and relished the quietness of his car as he began the drive to visit some of the shops he'd visited his last trip and considered maybe he shouldn't, with the description out, though he did wear a cap and heavily tinted glasses, but reconsidered. Maybe going into one of those shops, just to see how people reacted might prove helpful, and decided which one.

He walked in to find the place busier than before, but not crowded and no one gave him any attention. He stepped up to a lady he assumed worked there, he'd seen her before. "Do you have any old medical equipment or implements?" he asked.

She squinted in thought. "Can't recall seeing anything like that and not sure if we did where the heck it'd be, to tell you the truth."

"Thanks anyway," he said. She'd made eye contact, showed nothing of concern. "I'll just look around a bit."

"Help yourself." She went back to her task.

He saw the young girl, the right age, so it appeared, the right features, though pale and maybe too thin. She also had thick glasses, clearly poor eyesight, and all combined would normally be a deterrent, but there was something compelling about the sight of her that would not allow him to look away or discount her as a selection. She was peculiar in her manner of dress, wearing a neat skirt and blouse, looking much like the girls looked when he was a child, like in Sunday School. He knew he'd not be able to do anything inside and not likely outside either. Following people around was dangerous, even in a big city. He sensed the urgency rise and didn't want to draw attention, left and sat in his car, pondering over the matter. He watched the lady and two girls as they exited the shop. She could be the mother of the older girl, who was also pale and thin, but wholly different in appearance than the younger girl, who didn't look to be related, but he imagined she could look like her father.

It came to him that his strong urge towards this girl could be the very reason he couldn't discontinue his search. Maybe, he both hoped and considered, this was the very one he'd expected, and if so, he couldn't stop now and decided he'd follow them. He doubted his skills to pull it off, but the urge was too strong.

They entered a food mart and pulled next to the gas pumps. Without another idea he pulled in also, but the next entrance, around the corner. The older girl had gone into the mart while the woman pumped the gas, leaving the younger one in the car. He couldn't see her and knew even if she got out he could do nothing and questioned the saneness of his actions. He'd never felt so drawn to immediately and foolishly act, but he had to wait to be successful and understood the best thing to do would be to leave, but he couldn't.

The lady was back in the car, the older girl came out carrying two plastic bottles of some drink and they left. He gave them a few seconds and followed, saw them turn and hastily counted three streets ahead, to the left. He took that turn and they're still on the same road, as the houses become farther apart until it appeared they'd come upon a semi-rural area. They turned again and pulled up to a modest ranch style home on a street by itself, he estimated one hundred and fifty yards off the road he was on, and realized he didn't know the name of it. He traveled half a mile, parked and waited, gave them time to enter the home. He made the choice to return home but not before noting the street on which they lived, Bradford Lane, and the road that turned off the highway, Elderberry.

With the location known he could now return home.

Amy Louise peered through the small opening in the drapes and watched the car drive by, still unable to make out the driver's identity, but suspected she knew.

166

"What's wrong?" Linda asked.

"Someone followed us home," she said and let go of the drapes. "A man in a gray car followed us home, I think from the antique shop. He stopped when we got gas and followed us home."

"Are you sure?"

She nodded she was. "I think you should tell Poppa when he gets home."

"I'll call him now. I'm not waiting."

She keyed in his number, she got a recording and ended to call but he called back almost instantly.

"Bill, some man followed us home."

It was silent from Bill's end.

"We were at an antique shop and he followed when we left, stopped when we got gas and followed us home."

"You're certain?" He knew she was, but asked anyway.

"Yes, completely."

"How long ago did this happen?"

"He drove down Elderberry and turned around and passed the house going back to the highway maybe ten minutes ago."

"I'll call you back," Bill said with urgency. "I've got to make a quick call. Can you describe the car?"

Without waiting to be asked Amy Louise said, "Gray, it was a gray car."

"Bill, it was a gray car."

"What make, or style, anything else that'd help?"

Linda looked at Amy Louise, Elaine standing to her side. "Do you know the make of the car, who made the car or anything about it?"

"It was a gray car is all I know and it was like a family kind of car, with doors for the back seat."

"Bill, it was a gray sedan, four door. That's all we've got."

He said nothing and the call ended.

He wasted no time and called the number to contact Belinda Swafford with the information and she exhibited the same urgency as Bill's. "Thanks Bill, I let you know."

She dialed Cathy Stevens' number.

"Cathy, Belinda, listen, no time to waste, the suspect on the child abduction may have just left Landers and on his way home, it's a gray sedan, four door. That's all we've got."

"Okay, I'll be in touch." She ended the call, looked to an expectant Hearns. "The guy just left Landers; maybe headed our direction."

"We'll need help."

"You head for forty and I'll call it in."

Hearns was already picking out a spot to turn around, Stevens flipped on the siren and grill lights and called in for assistance. She and Hearns would cover the interstate and others would watch the two state highways coming from that direction, unless he took some out of the way route home they should have it covered, there wasn't time to do more and she took a deep breath, slowly exhaled, hoped it would be enough. Her adrenalin was beginning to wildly pump and knew Hearns' kicked in instantly.

Hearns calculated the spot providing the right overview and they reached it in what was likely about twenty minute. He knew it was about a forty-minute drive from Landers to Markham and knew some time had been lost, maybe fifteen minutes. So it'd be close. Stevens confirmed that the other two were in place.

As the minutes ticked away a sickening thought came to Stevens, that this may not be the guy they're looking for and all this hopeful anxiety would be for nothing. She glanced at Hearns and knew he wasn't short on hope. He could be like a little boy with his positive expectations, which she found both endearing and annoying. She noted the time on the dash and they'd been parked for over twenty minutes and it didn't feel good in the least, not to her and even Hearns had deflated some.

"What do you think?" she asked.

"He might've stopped for gas, or anything. We wait it out, maybe another hour."

She knew he was irritated and could hear it in his voice when he radioed the other units to hold tight for another hour. Deflated hope was often more painful than no hope at all, but only for a short time.

Nothing was worse than complete hopelessness, though she couldn't remember a moment of having experienced that, but knew it had to be the worse.

Carroll Grist bit into the juicy peach and considered it nearly perfect in its texture, firmness and sweetness. He's glad he chose to swing out of the way, to stop by the roadside vendor who sold various vegetables and fruit, and peaches were just coming in season. It was the right time to buy.

He bought a half a bushel and it was beyond his ability to wait until arriving home to bite into one, though the juice would run down his chin and maybe onto his shirt. After his denied expectations and the sight of the young girl in Landers he could think of no better consolation and distraction for his mind.

He knew where they lived – where she lived. That was enough to keep the despair away.

With one peach consumed, he greedily eyed the pile and chose another.

CHAPTER THIRTEEN

Larry Davis had waited over an hour to deliver his report to Alton Duncan, who walked in casual, unrushed, and he reigned in his irritation, knowing it was purposely done.

"Sorry you had to wait. I was in the middle of something," Duncan said as he poured a drink. He raised a glass toward Davis. "You want one?"

He was anxious to get this over with.

"No, thanks."

"What've you got?"

"A guy by the name of Uly Stevenson brings the kids and delivers to our man, John Edwards. Mack and Eddy Clements are the proprietors and their man in the field on the other end is Arn Knotts. So far I've not made a connection between them and this abduction thing."

"Have you talked with anyone?" Alton asked.

He shook his head. "No one. Wasn't sure if it was the thing to do, at least up front."

Alton nodded his agreement. "Pull this Arn Knotts fella aside and have a chat with him. He'll have a better feel since he's closely connected to that end."

"What if he's not cooperative?"

"It's not an option. We need to know."

Davis shrugged, lingered, thinking there would be more instruction and there wasn't, so he left. It was two days of misconnections before he had a conversation with Knotts who didn't sound like a willing subject.

"Look," Knotts said, "I'm just a mule, that's all, Mack and Eddy, they're the ones you need to talk to."

"No, you're the one I want to talk to. Do you or do you not know if there's any connection between the child abduction thing in the news and any of your sources?"

"Where do you think these people get them, from trees in an orchard? Like I said, I'm just the pickup and delivery man and it never pays for me to know too much."

"It's not going to be profitable for you to give me anything but a simple yes or no, even if it's a hunch."

"I'm not sure I like your threats."

"You'll like the real thing a lot less. Yes, or no?"

"I mean, I guess it could be, this ..."

"I asked for yes or no, not an I guess it could be."

"Let me finish, then you take decipher it as yes or no. This one guy I pick up from he's definitely in the right area and he's a bit weird. But then ain't they all?"

"His name?"

"I really don't like spouting out stuff like this, it's not kosher, and I don't want to lose my job."

"Losing a job ain't the worse thing in the world, jobs can be found. Health, like they say, if you got your health you got everything. Same thing could be said about life, without that you can't work."

"Man, I don't like the way this is going."

Davis looked up, his right hand massaging his taut neck, eyes peering over his nose at Knotts, and released a big sigh.

"Ok, let's go with yes and his name is ..." He realized he didn't know the man's name, only called him Birdman. "Look, I'm not lying on this, but I don't know his name. But I can give you an address, that's it."

"That'll do." He reached into his inside jacket pocket, took out a small pad and handed it and a pen to Knotts. "Write it down on this."

"Now, if I can remember the address," Knotts softly said to himself. "You know how it is, you go there, you know where it is and you don't think about the fact you really don't know the address."

"No, I don't know nothing like that, but I do know that if you don't come up with the correct information soon we may have to take another route."

"If you keep on with this strong arm stuff, you know, it's stressing me out, I'm never gonna remember the address."

Davis shook head with impatience.

Knotts looked up into the night sky and tried to draw the information from his anxious brain.

"Okay, the street is Laurel Drive, that I remember, but I swear to you I don't think I'll be able to give you the number without driving by the place."

"Then we drive by the place."

"Now, me and you?"

"Yeah, now, me and you." Davis could tell this didn't set well with Knotts. "Look, all I want is the information. I've got nothing to gain by doing you harm. I'll bring you back here safe and sound and you and I never see one another again. Promise."

Knotts appeared to relax a bit, nodded and followed Davis to his car. Something deep inside told him he needed to run but knew the uselessness of it. His daddy used to tell him if you hang out with thieves don't go complaining when they steal from you, and he wasn't sure how but in a round about way that sentiment applied to this situation.

He gave Davis general directions, his mind frantic, trying to come up with possible scenarios and how he'd handle them. Now he gave detailed directions and finally pointed to the location. "That's it, right there, where the guy lives."

"Looks like a business to me? He lives there too?"

"Yeah, he does."

"Complete computer repair and services." Davis read what was the closest thing to a sign. "You're not leading me astray here?"

"No, this is the place, for real."

Davis nodded and said nothing else, took Knotts back to his car, pulled up and silently waited for him to get out. It wasn't until he drove off that Knotts felt relieved, not expecting it to go so easy and concluded this might be a good time for a career change, maybe a long distance move, settle down and get a real job, even find a woman. He knew none of that would happen, except maybe the career change. He'd need to think about that one.

Carroll Grists' excitement grew as he anticipated his arrival in Landers. The girl's face remained fixed in his mind and he was certain this would be the one, the one he'd waited for. Even the flickering of the sunlight through the tall, straight pines wasn't an annoyance, almost enjoyable as they metered off the pace. He was careful to keep at the speed limit. He couldn't take chances being stopped for any reason, not today, it was too important.

His mind was restless, pushing him, and knew he had to settle it to avoid stumbling into a bad move or decision. He glanced at the dash that read seven forty-five and decided to stop for breakfast.

He had plenty of choices of places to sit, not many in yet, but he picked a table distanced from the largest in the dining room. The waitress wasn't fully awake and her hair disheveled, but was friendly. He ordered two eggs, over medium, hash brown potatoes and toast with coffee. She brought the coffee and he slowly sipped it, thinking about all that could happen later in the day, which wasn't serving the purpose of settling or slowing down his thoughts, so he thought about Kaye Fowler.

Not given to extreme curiosity he did find the possibilities interesting, of what could have happened to her to bring the noticeable change, at least one he could see. Of course, there's no way to know and likely no way to find out, but it did give some eerie consolation to his own twisted desires, to think they weren't that different, not really, and if not that different then he wasn't so isolated in his peculiarity.

The waitress setting the food on the table drew him back to the moment and he nodded to her as she asked, "Anything else?"

"No, thank you, this is fine."

"You need anything just let me know."

He smiled and again nodded as she swiftly left. He took his time with the meal, thought again of Kaye but pushed it aside, knowing there was nothing else to consider, wondered if today would be successful and resigned himself to being consumed with that agenda: Finding the girl.

⟫⟪ ⟫⟪

"Bill, we got a leak under the sink," Linda Bradford said into the phone.

He took off his cap and ran his fingers through his hair. "I'm tied up right now and can't get away, put something under it, to catch the water."

"I did but it seems to be getting worse and I need to run some errands."

It was quiet on Bill's end for a second. "Just turn the water off and I'll call Harris and get him over there later."

"I don't know how to turn the water off, I've never done it before."

"Out by the road is a round metal cover, it's over the meter, on the side of the meter is a valve, turn it counterclockwise to turn it off."

"I understood the part about the round metal cover and it's over the meter. Past that I'm lost." She heard him sigh into the phone.

"Inside the mudroom, beside the hot water tank is a long iron bar with a u-shaped end …"

She interrupted. "Hang on, let me look." Seconds passed. "Okay I've got it."

"Take that and go out to the meter and take the cover off. I'll wait."

Almost two minutes passed. "Okay, I've got it off and I see the meter, if it's got numbers on top."

"It does. Now look to the left of the meter and you see and turn valve and the u-shaped end fits over it. Turn it counterclockwise until it stops."

"Counterclockwise?"

"Think about the direction a clock goes and go the other way."

"I'm feeling dumb here." She laughed. "Okay I did that."

"You're doing fine. Go inside and turn on the water and see if it is off."

A minute passed. "Yes, it's off."

"Okay, I'll get Harris over later to fix the leak. You'll have to do without water until then."

"It'll have to be after three cause I've got some things to do."

"I'll tell him that. I've got to go, talk you to later."

She was about to say thanks but realized he was gone.

Bill ended the call and noticed Kenny had come in. He nodded and smiled.

"That Linda?" asked Kenny.

"Yeah. Got some plumbing problems."

"You know I've never knew how to turn the water off and figured it was out there at the meter, like you said to Linda."

"Not everyone does. I'll tell Linda you didn't know how either. It'll make her feel better, you know, knowing not everyone does."

Kenny smiled and nodded. "I went out to the fairgrounds, checked on progress, make sure all was in order."

"And?" asked Bill.

"All in order and they've about go it all set up. Maybe another day and they'll have it. Fair starts Sunday."

"I look forward to fall," Bill said. "But we've not had a bad summer."

"No, we've not. What're you tied up with?"

"Tied up with?"

"Yeah. You told Linda you were tied up with something and couldn't get out there."

"Oh, yeah," he said with urgency and grabbed and large envelope. "I got to run this over to the court house. Rachel called and said they needed some information on that accident that happened out near Darrell's place."

"You want me to run it over? I can."

"Naw, I got it. Just hang tight here until I get back."

Kenny shrugged and watched Bill hurry out and saw the paper, looked for the comics.

⊷ ⊶

Carroll Grist was curious as he watched her walk at a quick pace toward the curb, carrying what looked like a cane that had to be heavy judging by the way she carried it. She stopped, leaned over and gazed at something on the ground, stooped and lifted a circular metal object and let it fall upside down beside what must be a hole in the ground and stared down into it and was talking to someone on a phone. She placed the end of the cane into the hole and turned it. He then realized, or suspected, what was happening as he remembered that water meters were located in the ground, covered by a round metal lid and the cane was not a cane but was a metal tool of sorts for turning the water valve on and off. After using the metal tool she went into the house and didn't return. He thought through the situation, assuming she had issues with the water inside the house and may not be going out for the day, at least not for a while, and considered leaving and decided to wait thirty minutes with nothing else on the day's agenda. He saw the three walk out of the house and knew his waiting was the right choice.

He let them drive out of sight before beginning the careful pursuit, almost waited too long, lost sight of them and had to pick up speed to catch them. He slowed, followed them into town and watched as they stopped at a small grocery and knew based on the volume of business and excess of activity this would be a poor place to make his attempt. He passed the grocery and drove around the block, saw the car still in the lot, parked on the far side and waited. He followed them from the grocery to a medical office that housed several doctors and medical services. The lot was full and it was easy for him to hide as he waited.

Amy Louise was careful not to look too long in the direction of the following car, the same one that she'd seen before. It had followed them from home, to the grocery and then to the doctor.

Her mind was now on Elaine's visit with her doctor and anticipated the good news. She could tell Elaine was relaxed, but Mom looked anxious and when she squeezed her hand for assurance she gave her a nervous smile. She wondered how long it'd take before she understood.

In less than ten minutes Elaine was called back, with Linda and Amy Louise following, waited as formalities were finished and they were led to the examination room to wait for the doctor's arrival.

Doctor Williamson, a man of average height and weight, young and with sad eyes, arrived with other issues on his mind, or so it appeared, until he saw Elaine, and his expression went from confusion, to surprise, to happiness in less than a second, yet he only asked Elaine, "How are you feeling?"

"I'm feeling very good, I'm stronger, I can tell."

The doctor quickly glanced at Linda and back to Elaine. "Yes, you are looking well." He cleared his throat, hesitated and pondered his next statement. "I have here," he said holding up the papers, "the schedule for your next series of treatments." He leaned back and rubbed his chin. "How do you feel about beginning these treatments," he asked Elaine.

"I don't think I need them." She glanced at Linda who frowned and looked at the doctor, then back to Elaine.

"I think the doctor knows what is best," Linda weakly said with uncertainty. "Do you think she needs these treatments?" she asked the doctor.

He took a deep breath and let it out slowly. "With the information I have here," he said and nodded to the papers in his hand, "I'd say they're needed. So, yes."

"But she's better now," Amy Louise said, surprising the doctor and Linda and both looked at her like they just now became aware she was in the room.

"Yes," Elaine agreed, "I'm better now."

"But ..." Linda started to object when the doctor interrupted.

"Let me look at some things, see if it warrants more testing, then we'll decided if the treatments should be started.

"Is it wise," Linda inquired, "to wait too long on something like this."

"I'll do the preliminaries today, have the results day after tomorrow and we'll go from there." He stopped and looked at Elaine, then back to Linda. "If you want to start the treatments while we do the testing we can do that, if you'll feel better."

"Don't do the treatments," Elaine said. "Either way, I don't want the treatments."

Linda was distressed and looked back and forth between the doctor and Elaine. "Do the testing, then we decide," she said with resigned determination.

The doctor nodded. "I'll set things up and we'll take some blood and go from there."

The blood was drawn, an appointment set up for Thursday and they left the doctor's office without discussion and the mood coming from Linda was solemn.

It wasn't until they were in the car that anyone spoke, and it was Elaine. "Don't worry, Mom, it's going to be fine. I don't need the treatments, you'll see."

Linda glanced into the overhead rearview mirror and saw Amy Louise, felt the anger and didn't know why. Maybe she really did think Amy Louise was influencing things in the wrong direction. She'd not react to anything right now and wait until the results of the blood work came back. It was only two days delay, she thought for consolation.

Silence dominated the interior of the car for the longest time until Elaine asked, "Aren't we going to the library?"

"I thought we'd just go home. We can go to the library another time."

"My book is due today," Elaine said. "There'll be a fine."

Linda wanted to explode but instead turned and headed to the library, by the time they'd arrived she'd calmed and regretted her loss of control.

Elaine returned her book and went to the nonfiction section to search for another while Linda picked up a magazine and sat at a table and read while waiting.

"May I get a library card?" asked Amy Louise.

"Yes, but not today. Pick out a book and Elaine can check it out for you and we'll get you one next time." She desperately wanted to get home.

Amy Louise went to nonfiction and looked for a book as Linda watched with fascination, thinking she would've gone to the children's section.

The man on the next aisle was the man who'd been following them, though she'd not seen him up close, still she knew. She'd decided to not check out the book, this was more important. She pretended to scan section after section, moved toward the man, turned the corner, entered the same aisle and he looked uncomfortable. This increased when she stood beside him. She pulled a book from the shelf and appeared to be reading the inside cover and he stepped down, away from her, a few sections. She replaced the book to the shelf, walked past him and stood on the other side, pulled out another book and pretended to read the inside cover. He quickly left to the next aisle and she waited a few seconds, walked around and stood next to him.

"Do you want me to go with you?" she asked the man, who was startled by the question.

He looked at her as she stared up at him but didn't say anything.

"I'll go with you if you promise not to hurt anyone, not to hurt my sister or my mom."

He knelt down beside her. "You'll go with me, quietly?" His voice almost squeaked with excitement.

"Yes, I promise I will and I'll not make a fuss."

"Okay," he cautiously stated, imagined there must be a trick, or a trap, or something. "I'm going to walk out the side door, in the children's department and you follow me out to my car, staying behind me a bit."

She didn't say anything, only nodded she understood and he left with her following about ten steps behind. He was outside at his car and she stood at the passenger door, waiting. He stepped around as he remotely unlocked the doors, opened the door, said nothing as she slid into the seat and immediately reached for the seatbelt. Within minutes he was out of sight of the library and was having a hard time reconciling what'd just happened.

"Why did you do that?" he asked without look at her.

"You were going to take me anyway. Weren't you? I didn't want anyone to get hurt if a scene developed."

He wondered what kind of little girl talked like that, reasoned in that manner and came along willing knowing, or even suspecting, he was the person abducting children.

"Aren't you afraid?" he asked.

"Are you?"

He didn't expect that. "I'm not the one who should be afraid, it's you. Are you afraid?"

"Anyone who does the bad things you've done should be the one afraid. I'm not the one who've done those things, you are. Are you afraid?"

This was unsettling and becoming annoying, and he wasn't going to play word and mind games with a girl who likely was no more than eight years old. He focused on his driving and ignored her but continued to feel her eyes on him.

"What's wrong with you?" she asked.

"What do you mean, wrong with me? Why I do what I do?"

"No, why you don't have hair?"

"I shave my head."

"No. It's not that, I can tell, you don't have any eyebrows or eyelashes, no hair on your arms." She paused, her forehead furrowed with concern. "What's wrong with you?"

"It happened when I was young, something traumatic and afterwards it all came out."

"I'm sorry that happened."

She sounded sincere but he didn't know how to respond so he again ignored her and still felt her eyes on him.

"The bad thing that happened to you, it was from an accident or did someone hurt you."

"It was from an accident." He sighed heavily. "Could you ride in silence?"

"I could." He heard what sounded like humor in her voice. "Do you want me to?"

"Yes, if you don't mind just sit quietly."

"You smell good," she stated.

He wondered what could be wrong with the girl and refused to respond.

"If I had to pee would you stop?"

"Do you have to pee?"

"No. I only want to know if I do if you'll stop."

"Yes, if you need to pee I'll stop."

"What if I'm hungry?"

He shook his head but was amazed how little annoyance he felt. "Are you hungry?"

"Yes, I am hungry and probably when I eat and drink something I'll have to pee so if we stop one time that will be enough."

The statement struck him as humorous, or he thought it might be humor, he wasn't sure, but it was comical, intended or not, and he hoped he'd not smiled. But it wouldn't hurt if she saw him smile and could work to his advantage by calming any anxiety she might have, though he was certain she had none. Again, he considered, what was wrong with this girl that she'd behave in such a way in this circumstance. It wasn't right.

"Are we going to stop?" she asked after a few moments.

He was not going to answer her and imagined she was trying to work some kind of control thing on him and he wasn't going to play into her hand and then found it odd that he imagined such a young girl could be playing him. He saw a Wendy's ahead.

"You like Wendy's?"

"I like some things Wendy's has, but not every thing they have so I'll have to order my own because I'm pretty choosy about what I eat. I don't want to be a bother, but I'm pretty choosy."

He shook his head and considered just leaving her at Wendy's. He recalled that this was the little girl he had previously thought was the special one, the one that would make the difference in his life that would change everything and questioned how he could've considered that, but then, she was different and different could be special, so he'd not leave her at Wendy's.

He couldn't help but think of the oddness of he and the little girl standing at the counter like normal people and ordering at Wendy's but he knew she'd not make a scene. Why he knew that he wasn't sure, but he knew.

After the meal, she went to the restroom on her own and returned with a look of anticipation.

"I'm ready," she said.

Without direction or assistance she entered the car, buckled up and pulled her skirt so the seatbelt would not overly crease it, looked over at him and smiled.

He shook his head and was overwhelmed, almost to eeriness, at the unusual state of this whole thing. He was both thinking on this weird situation and focusing on his driving when he felt the girl's hand on his bare arm, which he pulled away.

"What are you doing?" he asked with suspicion.

"I wanted to see how smooth your arm was without hair on it. It's smooth as mine. Did you know that? You want to feel my arm to see how smooth it is?" She held up her arm and gazed with invitation.

"No, I don't. Just stay over there and sit still and be quiet until we get ..." He stopped because he was going to say home, but that didn't seem to fit and didn't finish the thought.

He didn't look her way but could tell she sat up straighter in the seat and was quiet for the longest time, during which time he continued to notice an oddness lingering in his mind, almost a calm, with order, and he felt relaxed. He had no explanation and was unable to recall feeling that way during his adult life, only as a child, and not to this level. He refused to admit his mind was toying with the idea the girl may be the source, the explanation for this new thing. Maybe the social interactions of the evening had initiated those new and strange feelings. He wasn't accustomed to social interactions and if the girl had any effect it was for that reason.

She remained quiet for the rest of the trip and was asleep when they arrived.

He pulled into the garage and looked at her sleeping, leaning against the door, and couldn't understand what was happening, why he felt as he did, why he wanted to take care of her, to protect her, to help her. Now came a feeling with which he was familiar: Confusion.

CHAPTER FOURTEEN

Cathy Stevens looked at her phone to check the time. Belinda Swafford, the epitome of punctuality, was late.

David Hearns watched as she did and asked. "How late is she?"

"Ten minutes," she said and saw her coming down the hall. Even from a distance she looked haggard and walked in looking worse.

"You look like you might be running late to your own funeral," Hearns said.

"It's not funny," Belinda said with a half smile. "I'm thinking death might be an improvement, surely couldn't hurt as bad."

"Maybe you need to take some time off," Stevens said. "See a doctor, something. You look horrible."

"Well looks aren't deceiving." She set her case on the table and slowly eased into the chair, leaned all the way back and let out a large, noisy sigh.

"What is it, the flu?" Hearns asked.

"Nope, it's some sort of stomach bug or food poisoning." Both hands combed through her hair. "Enough about me, let's get started on this abduction thing. Can you believe it, Bill Bradford's daughter a victim?"

"Well, this is a girl they'd recently taken in," Steven said, "with the intent of eventually adopting her."

Belinda looked surprised. "Didn't know that part. He's got a daughter, right, and she's sick or something?"

"Yes, with leukemia, up in her young teens, or so I think," Steven said. "The girl who was taken was a nine years old, Amy Louise Crawford."

Belinda read through her notes. "Taken Wednesday, from city library, no one saw anything, one lady in the library reported seeing an odd man. What's this odd man?"

"She said an odd looking man, one she'd never seen before, was in the library," Hearns said. "That's it, no one saw the odd looking man doing anything wrong."

"What made the guy odd looking, his manner, actions, what?"

"She said he was just odd looking and was a stranger to the person who saw him," Hearns said.

"So we've got nothing to tie this odd looking man to anything? Did this lady see the posted description of the suspect? "

"She did," Stevens said. "But couldn't be certain, said he had a cap and glasses, the picture had neither."

"She was with her mother ... well, Bill's wife?" asked Belinda.

"Yes, she and their daughter, Elaine and this Amy Louise had gone to the library," Steven said. "When they got ready to go she was gone. They made a thorough search. Folks at the library helped, but she wasn't found."

"Bill's wife, Linda," Hearns said, "is not taking it well at all. Keeps saying it's her fault. You know how those things go."

Belinda nodded she did and Stevens shook her head in sympathy.

"What about a picture of the girl?" Belinda asked.

"The lady who runs the place where the girl stayed, Raylene Niles, is sending a recent photo, so we may have it today," Hearns said.

"Raynetta," Stevens said.

"Uh?" Hearns asked.

"Here name is Raynetta Niles."

"Anyway, we'll get her picture out tomorrow, along with the others."

"Excuse me," Belinda said as she hastily left the room, nearly trotting down the hall.

"She needs to see a doctor," Hearns stated.

"Yep, but doubt she will," Stevens said. "You know how she is."

He shrugged. "I'll take your word on it, but she needs to see a doctor."

"When was the last time you saw a doctor?" asked Stevens. "Outside the annual check-up we have to do?"

"I just never get sick," Hearns smugly said.

"Yeah, like last winter when you …"

He stopped her. "Okay, I know what you're going to say."

Stevens grinned in victory as Belinda returned.

"Sorry about that," she said. "I think I'm gonna have to break down and see a doctor. You know a good one?"

"The guy we see on the annual physicals is a good one," Hearns said.

"Think he can see me today?" she asked. "Cause I'm about done for here."

"I'll be right back," Stevens said and left.

Belinda sat, leaned forward, her head in both hands while Hearns sat uncomfortably waiting for Stevens' return that was five minutes later.

"He said to come on over," Stevens said to Belinda. "We'll drive you."

It was obvious she wasn't going to argue. Hearns dropped off Stevens and Belinda at the doctor's office and left to check on the update of the picture of the newly abducted girl. It had arrived via computer and he relayed it to the local station for broadcast as soon as possible and texted Stevens, asked her to let him know when they were ready. He didn't like doctors or their offices.

Carroll Grist woke that morning, but it wasn't like any other morning, because he woke with that girl on his mind and realized he didn't know her name. He'd never known the name of any of the others and considered why he thought about her differently, unless it was because she was that one, the one who'd make the difference. Or, it could simply be how strange she was. Maybe that was why he woke thinking of her, her peculiar manner. Even her appearance was peculiar, dressing like a little doll from the fifties. It was the next realization that bothered him the most: He was lying in bed and smiling.

Quickly he rose and dressed, forced his attention on the routine of the morning and put that girl out of his mind. Remembering that he didn't sedate her caused him a mild bit of concern, but not much. She'd not been any trouble and he didn't expect her to become any. He made coffee and drank one cup before unlocking and knocking on the door. He cracked a one-inch opening and spoke through it, "I'm coming in."

He heard no response and found her sitting on the edge of the bed, as if she'd been like that all night.

"Did you sleep?"

"Yes, I did, a little but not much."

"Are you hungry?"

"I am hungry." She slid off the bed. "I don't like wearing the same clothes two days in a row – I was not prepared to be abducted."

"I'm sure you'll be fine," he said and suppressed a grin.

"I'm sure I'll not suffer greatly having to wear the same clothes two days in a row but I have to be honest and say that I doubt I'll be fine."

Ignoring the clothes issue, he asked, "What would you like to eat?"

"I'd like oatmeal if that's possible."

He thought. "I don't have any oatmeal, I have Raisin Bran."

"I'm not fond of cold cereals." She looked at him with resignation. "But Raisin Bran will be okay."

"Maybe we can go out and find you some clothes," he said for consolation.

She shook her head in amazement.

"What?" he asked.

"I'd imagine they have a picture of me on the TV by now and you can't take me with you to buy my clothes and I'm sure you'll not do very well on your own. I'm fairly ..."

"I know," he interrupted. "You're particular."

She nodded.

"You eat then we'll figure out what to do next."

"How long are you going to keep me?"

He hadn't come up with a plan, shrugged but didn't say anything.

"What are you going to do with me?"

"Something has come up, a change of plans, and I've not yet determined how I'm going to work this out. That'll be one of the things I'll have to figure out next."

What he did know was he was not contacting Arn, but that put him in a difficult dilemma. What to do with this girl?

"What did you do with the rest of them?" she asked and watched the darkness fall over his face.

He pushed his bowl away, got up and left he room.

Amy Louise continued eating and soon finished her cereal, took both bowls to the sink and wiped clean the table and returned to the room to wait.

Several hours passed, she had no clock in the room, could tell he busied himself with what she supposed was work. She'd seen the computers and related items and understood what his business likely involved. She heard a new voice, a man's, and listened intently but couldn't make out the conversation, eased out of the door and peered undetected around the corner and saw what she assumed was a business discussion. She returned to the room to wait and wondered what the day would bring, if he was going to ignore her for hours but experienced no anxiety from the uncertainty.

No more than another hour had passed and she heard another voice, this time it was a woman. She again slipped out, eased down and peered around the corner, quickly pulled back when she saw the lady make eye contact with her. She hurried back to the room, sat on the edge of the bed and considered this new development.

Kaye Fowler braked hard and stopped only feet away from the city bus and was now aware she needed to focus more on driving than the new developments in the investigation. Since the last visit from the two detectives, to inform her they were off the case and new ones would be taking over. She'd heard nothing and the nothing bothered her and she struggled to be optimistic.

She parked on the side of Carroll Grist's shop and thought on the close call, the hard stop just experienced, was glad it'd happened before she picked up the repairs, else there may have been damage.

She entered to find no one in the front room, which was common since it was her understanding he did most of the repairs in the larger room off to the side of the building, also knowing he lived somewhere in the complex, yet unfamiliar with the layout. These were only thoughts to pass time until he came out, which he did, but looked different. She wasn't sure what it was, but he looked different.

He stepped out, saw it was Kaye. "Hang on. I'll be right back."

She nodded her acknowledgement, assumed he went to pick up the items for which she'd come. She pondered on exactly what was different about Carroll and the best she could conclude is that he looked relaxed, definitely not his normal demeanor.

He came out, set the packages on the low table. "You need help carrying them out?" he asked.

"No, that's fine, I can get it."

He looked through the various items over the top of the counter and picked up a gray pad, opened it and looked grimly at the page. "I have a total here, but I don't have the breakdown ready." He looked up with question. "I can email the breakdown later, maybe this afternoon, or tomorrow?"

"That'll work, definitely not a problem," she said and thought she's never heard him string that many words together.

"The Dell had more problems than suspected."

"Whatever you've done I know it was necessary, no explanations needed."

He turned around and looked through a stack of paper, lifting one, looking, then to another.

Kaye caught sight of a girl, a small girl who'd stepped out, made eye contact and looked like she'd been found out in some act of mischief, and instantly returned from where she'd come. She thought it odd, first that anyone would be here and least of all a young girl and pushed it out of her mind since it wasn't her business and was likely family.

Carroll turned back to the counter, form in hand and handed it to Kaye. "This is a complete workup on the Dell. I'm not fully confident that I resolved all the issues, but if there are problems, let me know."

She nodded her understanding, amazed at the volume of words coming out of his mouth, and the over and above manner of assistance. "Thanks, Carroll. You didn't have to do that."

He almost smiled and shrugged. "Let me help you with those." He looked at the packages.

"Okay, but, really, I got them."

"This way you only have to make one trip."

It was after the packages were loaded and she was halfway back, it came to her like it burst into her brain. The girl, the one at Carroll's, she looked like one of the abducted girls, the most recent she believed. Yes, she was sure now, that if it wasn't it was someone who looked exactly like her. And why would he have a small girl in his home like that? She made the decision to turn around and thought of how the girl wasn't afraid and didn't look like someone in trouble, not that kind of trouble. She looked like she'd been caught in the act of some trouble, but not in trouble, and that was odd. Maybe she was going to make a fool of herself and didn't care. She had to do this.

She parked a block away, walked to the shop, slowly, deliberately walked around and inspected the windows, one by one. She saw evidence of movement in the one ahead, carefully looked into the window and saw Carroll speaking with the girl, impossible to make out any of the words, but the girl didn't look afraid and both seemed natural in their manner. Still, she had to be sure. Looking again at the girl she was more convinced.

She entered the front area and didn't wait for anyone, stepped behind the counter and walked toward the door from which the girl had previously come. Before she reached it Carroll stepped out looking confused.

"Kaye?" He paused. "Is there a problem?"

"I saw a girl. A small girl when I was here a few minutes ago and she looked like the one on TV, one of the abducted girls." There wasn't any accusation in her voice.

"You saw her?" He thought on it a second. "You think she looks like one of the girls that was abducted?"

She vigorously nodded. "Yes, I do. Who is that girl, Carroll?" she asked with a hint of accusation. "You've never been married, so you don't have children and you don't have brothers or sisters so it's not a niece." She waited for his response knowing the last part she made up, taking a stab at a probability.

He didn't have an answer, not one he could immediately spit out, and pondered over his options, what to say, or what to do.

Still without response he only looked at her, eye to eye.

She knew that look and also knew hesitation only made things worse. It was obvious he didn't expect what came. His legs out from under him and flipped him in onto his stomach. She was on his back, her knee causing pain that he didn't mind, but couldn't move.

"What are you doing, Kaye?" he asked without much strain and wondered how all happened so quickly.

"If that girl isn't one of the abducted girls then what I'm doing is making a serious mistake but I'm not one to take chances."

"Don't hurt him." The voice that was firm and polite startled her and its origin was the small girl. She looked even smaller up close, frail but still unafraid.

Kaye eased the pressure on Carroll's back and considered her next move. "Are you one of the girls abducted, the ones on TV?"

"I'll not tell you anything until you stop hurting him and let him get up."

She debated the sensibility of doing that and slowly eased off him. He didn't make an immediate effort to get up, but gradually stood, still confused, didn't look threatening toward her and the girl didn't appear to be in danger. She considered a big mistake may have been made, but wasn't going to show it.

"Are you on of those abducted girls?" she asked again.

"Yes, I am." The small girls walked closer. "But Mr. Carroll is being nice and helping me."

"Is he the one who took you?" She kept a careful eye on Carroll.

"He is helping me to get back home. So you don't have to be worried because everything is all right." The girl looked at Carroll who was still torn on how to respond as he dealt with a plethora of new emotions and thoughts he had no idea how to manage. The girl walked to his side and held his hand, which he accepted with a light squeeze.

"I don't feel right leaving you here," she said to the girl, looked at Carroll, back at the girl and closed her eyes, shook her head. "I don't know what's going on here but what I do know is that it's not right. Something here is wrong and I don't feel right leaving you here." She walked closer to them both and looked at the girl. "Why don't you go with me?"

"I don't know you."

She held out her hand to the girl. "Kaye Fowler. Glad to meet you."

"Amy Louise Crawford," she said and barely touched Kaye's hand. "Sorry, I don't know where it's been."

Kaye couldn't help but smile. "Right. You don't." She knelt down. "I promise I'm a good person who is only trying to help."

"You say you're a good person, and I think you want to help me, but you've done some things that some might not call so good."

Kaye stood, also confused and wondered if she understood, or maybe misunderstood.

Before she could respond the girl said, "You can go and not worry. I know Mr. Carroll, and I know you mean well, but he will take care of me."

She shrugged. "Okay." She still didn't feel like leaving was the right thing, not without the girl. "I'll go then." She turned, looked back at Carroll. "Sorry about that, Carroll."

He nodded his acceptance, eyes wide with a lot of things he clearly didn't understand.

The feeling that she shouldn't have left without the girl couldn't be shaken as Kaye drove away. What bothered her more was what the girl had said about her having done some things, things that others would not consider good. If was obvious she didn't know about her and those things she'd done. But, what else could that have meant?

An idea came, one she resisted and then relented, because she had to do something. She had to find those detectives but couldn't remember their names, rolled it around in her mind and searched for a way to contact them. The lady detective had left a card on the table but she couldn't remember what she'd done with it, even if she'd picked it up. Maybe, she considered, Greg had picked it up and a name popped into her head. Clark Daniels. She pulled into the lot of a closed dry cleaner and called Clark.

Explaining she needed the number of the two detectives raised his suspicion. "Why do you want their number?"

"I'll have to explain later. Do you have it?"

"You're not going to do something stupid are you?" he asked.

"What do you mean?"

"Your not going to confess, are you?"

"No, nothing like that, this isn't even related to that. It's about one of the abducted girls, the ones on TV."

"What about them?"

"Clark, honestly, this is important and there's no time to waste. I'll fill you in later. Promise."

"Hang on." He was gone a few seconds. "Okay, here it is."

She wrote it down and immediately made the call and it was the guy.

"Not sure you remember me," she stated. "Kaye Fowler. I need to meet with you as soon as I can. Is this possible?"

"Where are you?" he asked.

"On Dresher, about the sixteen hundred block, I think."

"Stay there. Give us ..." He paused. "Fifteen minutes."

John Edwards accompanied Larry Davis to make the call on the location pointed out by Arn Knotts. Davis noticed Edwards looked calm but he was anxious and tried to hide it. He was the lead man on this and had to prove his mettle.

The sun settled low in the late afternoon horizon as Edwards pulled into the location to which Davis had pointed, shifted into park and looked at Davis who nodded.

The front room was empty as the two men entered. Edwards stayed back, closer to the door as Davis stepped to the counter. He looked around for a way to get someone's attention, had not heard a sound when they entered, stepped to the far right of the counter and was about to go around when the man stepped out.

"Could I help you?" the man asked and Davis was momentarily distracted by his odd appearance.

"You know a man by the name of Arn Knotts?" Davis asked.

He shook his head. "Not a name that sounds familiar."

"Then the names Mack and Eddy Clements would also be unfamiliar?"

The guy nodded. "What's this about?"

"We're not cops if that's what you're worried about." He decided to go for broke. "We know Knotts picks up kids here so we can cut to the chase and bypass all that."

The tall man didn't show concern, but did step back one step. "Are you sure you've got the right person, the right place?" he asked.

"We do, and we don't have time to kill playing games." His confidence rose. "You're the guy taking them kids, the ones on TV?"

"Of course not."

Davis was running out of options and began to think maybe Knotts had pulled a fast one. Then he saw the girl standing at the end of the hall, just outside a doorway. He recognized her.

"Never mind." He moved in the direction of the girl. "We got our answer right here."

Instead of running away the girl rushed to the odd looking man and stood by his side. Davis had not considered this scenario, unsure what to do, grabbed the girl by the arm but wasn't prepared when the big guy come at him.

For a big man he wasn't that strong and Davis quickly gained control of the situation and looked back at Edwards. "Take the girl." Edwards moved quickly.

Davis inwardly debated if he should eliminate this guy or take him along. He looked again to Edwards. "Take the girl to the car."

"If you hurt him I promise I'll only cause trouble," the small girl stated without fear. "I promise, even if you hurt me, it won't matter, I'll only cause trouble."

Davis looked at the girl with amazed humor. "And if we don't hurt him?"

"Then I go without making a fuss. I'll be quiet and not make a fuss."

Davis quickly analyzed and knew the big guy wasn't going to the police, looked at Edwards. "Let's go."

"We leave the guy here?" asked Edwards.

"Yeah, what's he gonna do, call the police and point the finger at himself?"

Edwards was still concerned and thought the best move would be to not leave the guy alive, take all the money and it's looks like a robbery, and no one knows about the girl.

"You take the girl to the car," he instructed Davis.

Davis started to argue but saw Edward's eyes, took the girl and left.

They'd not yet entered the car and the shot was heard. Davis looked at the girl for her reaction and she showed none, but the look she gave made him feel oddly uncomfortable. He opened the back door and shoved the girl in and slid in behind her, had only buckled his seatbelt when Edwards jumped in and left in a hurry. No words were exchanged as they drove to meet with Alton Duncan.

Edwards looked into the review mirror over the dash, caught sight of the girl. "What kind of trouble did you plan to cause?"

She didn't respond.

"Guess it was a bluff," he stated and chuckled.

"It's not over," she said.

He cranked his head around and stared at the little girl and considered a response, one that didn't come to him. He shook his head and the trip was continued in silence.

CHAPTER FIFTEEN

The lights of the SUV flashed twice and Cathy Stevens pointed. "That must be her."

David Hearns pulled beside and waited while Kaye Fowler slipped into the back seat and wasted no time.

"I think I've found one of the girls who was abducted."

"Found?" asked Stevens.

"Yeah, this guy who does repair work for us, Carroll Grist, I went to pick up some stuff and I saw her there. I confronted him and the girl said she was fine with him … but it was her, I'm sure of it."

Stevens, deciphering the excited words, understood one thing: She'd spotted who she thought was one of the abducted children. "Which one was it, do you know?"

"The most recent one."

"Amy Crawford?"

"I don't remember a name, just the last one to show up, I think that's why it was fresh on my mind and she does have a peculiar look, sort of."

Hearns was already in motion. "Where is this guy?"

Kaye began with directions for the short drive and once inside no one was in the front room.

Kaye called out. "Carroll!"

A faint groan was heard and Stevens found him lying in blood behind the counter, began to do what she could while Hearns called for an ambulance and back up.

"He has a strong pulse," she called out.

Kaye stepped up to the counter, looked over and regretted the way she'd treated him earlier, even if he was maybe the abductor. She wasn't sure of anything and wished she could go back and do it differently.

Stevens hushed the room, though no one was saying anything, leaned in close to Carroll. "He said they took the girl." Her eyes pleaded. "Did you know who these people were?"

Arn Knotts was all she heard.

Alton Duncan was unhappy about the newly developed situation and the amateurish way it was handled. A good plan accounted for the unexpected and decisions should be made swiftly and uniformly. This was not the CIA or KGB, they were expected to operate on levels far above those and any like them. He suspected the problem could be Davis, newest to that level.

"Why did you bring the girl here?" Duncan asked Davis. "She's one of those on TV."

He hesitated on the response, affirmed Duncan's concerns about his indecisiveness. "There was no use for the guy, so we brought the girl."

Duncan didn't display his distress over that answer. "What happened to the guy?"

"I took care of him. It was covered," Edwards stated.

Duncan nodded his understanding, knowing 'covered' meant all company requirements were met and this satisfied him, at least concerning the task at hand. He still had matters to ponder concerning Davis.

He met the eyes of the child who was looking at him and her manner surprised him. He'd never seen one look so ... he considered the right word ... calm. Maybe, but there was something else, beyond calm. Confidence, she had a calm confidence. Maybe, he thought, Davis could learn from her.

"Edwards, accompany me as I take her back," Duncan said. "Davis, you're done for the day."

His tone told him there'd be a discussion later and hope he'd not be fired, not understanding that no one was fired from his position, only terminated.

The girl silently walked ahead, but Duncan had questions. "Things go okay with that?"

Edwards knew what 'that' meant. "Went okay, I suppose. It ended well, that's all that matters. Right?"

He didn't say anything, didn't make any acknowledge or confirm he thought all matters had ended well.

Seconds later, "Did Davis handle himself?" asked Duncan.

"Hard to say. He was a bit slow, indecisive, but like I said, we ended it well."

Duncan nodded, but Edwards knew it wasn't over and he hoped he would be out of the picture when the issues were addressed.

Amy Louise had no interest in the conversation and hoped they were taking her where the others were, stepped aside when they reached the first door. Passing through the last door they entered into a large room and she spotted two faces from those on the television. A few looked completely lost and hopeless and those who didn't had little spark in their eyes, but at the moment there were other matters to address.

She stepped up to and looked up at Edwards. "I'd like to go home."

He shook his head in mock amazement and smiled. "You'd like to go home," he said and grinned. "You gonna cause trouble now?"

She grabbed him by the hand, he made an effort to pull it away but found his strength instantly drained, weakened and barely able to stand he dropped to his knees and his heart stopped, he hit the floor and was dead. All happened so quickly he didn't have time to comprehend the experience of what had happened and reclined peacefully on the floor.

Duncan quickly recovered from the shock of what he'd witnessed, moved toward Amy Louise without clear intentions, acting on instinct that didn't provide a conclusive response. He reached for the girl as she intercepted his arm and grasped it at the wrist. He went to his knees, tried to analyze the situation but his mind was blurred. Almost totally paralyzed, had things to say but words wouldn't come.

"I have a message for you, for you to pass along to Moreland."

He could hear but was unable to express the shock he felt from those words, especially the name Moreland, a name known only among the seventy.

Knowing he was unable to respond she continued with the message she wanted relayed and release her grip as Duncan. Still on his knees, he fell and tumbled forward.

She waited, gave him time to began his recovery. "Do you understand the message?"

He didn't respond and tried to stand.

She waited for him to more fully recover as the others began to gather around, drawn by curiosity and hopefulness.

Duncan finally stood on his still wobbly legs, looked at the girl with an attempt at menace but failed to achieve it.

"Did you understand the message?"

He wouldn't respond and she stepped towards him as he shuffled back.

"If you didn't understand the message, I'll repeat it. Did you understand the message?"

He reluctantly nodded, his aggressions returning.

"It is important you deliver the message just as I gave it. Do you understand?"

"I understand this, that your life is worthless." His raspy voice was of one who was gravely ill.

"Then you should go and deliver it."

"I don't take orders from a little girl." He paused as his strength returned and anger quivered through his body. "I'm going, but not at your command."

He opened the door, stood holding it open and looked back. "You'll not get out of here, it's impossible."

He visually scanned the room, his eyes bulging with his passions. "Enjoy!" he yelled. "All of you, your last moments of life. When I return it will be the end for you all."

He loudly pulled the door shut.

They heard him as he passed through the next door with as much hostility.

All moved around Amy Louise who had walked to the body of Edwards, knelt down, reached inside this inside jacket pocket and pulled out his cell phone. She keyed in a number and casually waited for an answer.

"Mom, this is Amy Louise," she said to an instantly hysterical Linda. "I need your help, I need you to do something for me."

"Amy, are you alright?" She screamed the question.

"Yes, I am, but I need you to do something very important for me. It's very important."

Trying to calm her thoughts Linda asked, "What, what do you need me to do?"

"Write down this number, the one I'm calling from, and call Dad and give him that number, tell him to call the right people and he'll know who, tell him to give them that number and have them to call me. Do you understand?"

"Yes, I do understand." Some calm had returned. "Are you all right?"

"Yes, I'm all right. I love you and sorry you had to go through this."

"I love you too, Amy ..."

"Mom, it's important you make that call now. I'll be home, maybe tomorrow sometimes. We'll have plenty of time."

"Uh ... ok. Bye, Amy and I love you."

"I love you too." She ended the call and smiled to the group gathered around. "We're going home."

Linda called Bill and had to go through the relaying of information three times, once to get past his confusion, next to get past his disbelief and finally for him to get it.

He called Belinda, still recuperating, who immediately contacted Stevens and Hearns.

"Of all the oddest things," Stevens stated when Belinda passed along the information.

"What?" Belinda asked.

"I'll have to explain later."

Stevens ended the call and looked over to David and said with a can-you-believe-this tone. "That was Belinda. Amy Louise just called Bill's wife with a number for us to contact. She wants us to call her."

She keyed in the number.

"Is this a police officer?" Amy Louise asked when she answered.

"Yes, I'm Detective Cathy Stevens. Tell us what you need us to do?"

Amy Louise gave the specific directions to their location, having taken the time to note all the details.

"You will need help getting to us, there are several doors and they'll be hard to get through."

"Us?" Stevens asked. "You said us? Who is with you?"

"There are other kids here besides me, nine I think, and at least three are on the list of abducted kids."

Steven went breathless for a second, repeated the directions to Amy Louise as Hearns listened, adjusting his route. Kaye imagined she should be let out somewhere but no one acknowledged her presence in the back.

"Stay on the phone, I need to make a call for help."

"I've got it," Hearns said, holding up his phone. "They'll be able to track us by GPS."

"Did you let them know we've got some heavy barriers to get through?"

"Got it covered." Hearns looked to the back. "You okay back there?"

"For now," Kaye said. "You think this is a good idea, me along like this?"

"I think you can handle it," Stevens said as she shifted around to face the back. "You're a capable young lady. Right?"

"Yeah, I guess so. Right." The response was weak.

"You see that?" Hearns asked and Stevens shifted around and looked in the direction he pointed.

"The helicopter?"

"Yeah. Could've taken off from our point of destination. Call it in."

Stevens relayed the information as they arrived before the others.

Stevens shifted around to face Kaye. "You stay in the car."

"Good idea," she responded.

"Cavalry's here," Hearns stated as he opened his door and saw the beginnings of the arrival of backup.

"Don't worry. All is good," Stevens said to Kaye who nodded hopefully.

They stood outside, accessed the options and walked to what appeared to be the front entrance. Without expectation Hearns pushed on the lever and nothing happened.

"Need assistance," he called out.

The door opened without much effort, they entered and were clueless on the direction.

Stevens called Amy Louise. "We're inside. Which way now?"

Following her instructions they were soon at a secured door that took ten minutes to get through. Moving forward they come to another and then another, each giving them little trouble.

Stevens saw Amy Louise sitting on a stool, gazed around at the others who wanted to come but were still hesitant, cautious.

Amy Louise slipped off the stool and stood next to Stevens as Hearns walked past.

"It's okay," he said and knelt. "We're the police, all is okay and we're going to take you home."

Edward's body was quickly removed, officers worked through the group, one boy shivered and started to cry loudly and several quietly wept, some in mild shock. Names and relatives could be dealt with later, now the goal was to calm and reassure.

Stevens tried not to think about what these kids had gone through, what it would take to get them back to living a normal life, if it was even possible for all of them. Some looked emotionally detached. She looked down at Amy Louise and saw little emotion displayed, rather saw the confidence and satisfaction of an accomplished mission, having seen the same in fellow cops.

Still she asked, "You okay?"

Amy Louise nodded and said nothing.

"Hello?" The voice came from behind her and turned to find the lady from Mr. Carroll's shop but had forgotten her name.

"Did you tell the police about me being at Mr. Carroll's shop?"

"I did," she answered with apprehension. "I guess it was alright."

"It was." She paused in thought. "It helped too. Thank you."

"Is it okay," Kaye asked Stevens, who now had Hearns standing next to her, "if I speak with her alone." She nodded to Amy Louise.

Stevens and Hearns exchanged glances and he shrugged.

"Sure," Stevens said. "Go ahead, if it's okay with her."

"It's fine," she said

Waiting for the two to be out of hearing range she knelt beside Amy Louise. "You said something back at Mr. Carroll's about me having done things that others might think bad. What did you mean by that?"

She looked at Kaye with eyes that said it went without saying. "What's in the past can be just that, in the past, that is if you want them to be."

"Some things are hard to leave in the past, they tend to haunt you, pick at the scabs, not just for me, but for others. Maybe you just have to get rid of the ghosts that cause the pain."

Amy Louise gazed into her eyes with understanding, even nodded. "Yes, there's lots of pain, and I'm sorry you had to go through all that."

Kaye's eyes welled with tears. She grabbed Amy Louise, pulled her into her bosom and held her tight and felt the surge pass through and let go, leaned back, stared numbly into her eyes, unable to understand. Then the flood came and she fell to the floor sobbing, soon quieted and stretched out of the floor, on her side, tired and weak.

She was dizzy when she attempted to get up but required no explanation of what'd happened. All the past, the dark deeds, the horror, the pain, all were gone and she was free. She looked up to Stevens, who'd seen her distress, came and knelt beside her. They made eye contact and she knew what she had to do.

Stevens helped her up, Hearns stood back, uneasy, not sure what to do.

"Something I've got to do," Kaye began but was interrupted.

"Yes," Stevens said. "You need to go home, clean up and get some rest."

"No, you don't understand ..."

Stevens frowned, glared with concerned intensity. "I don't think you understand. You need to go home, clean up and get some rest."

Hearns had stepped closer and Kaye looked to him for help, but he only smiled and nodded. "Just do what she said."

She looked to Amy Louise and received a smile and a nod.

"I think I need to go home, clean up and get some rest."

"I'll have someone take you to your vehicle," Hearns said and stepped away.

She stepped up to Stevens and hugged her. "Thank you."

It was enough for her. "You're welcome."

She knelt down beside Amy Louise, started to hug her but decided against it. "Thank you so much." Amy Louise smiled at her caution.

"I don't understand what happened ..." She thought a second, decided to not say anything more and stood as Hearns walked up with the officer who'd drive her to her car.

Hearns and Stevens stood next to each other, shared a glance that said all that needed to be said. As if on cue they both looked to Amy Louise who was now the only child left in the room.

"You ready to go home?" asked Stevens.

"I am."

She walked to where they stood, stopped and looked around the room and continued her exit as Hearns and Stevens followed.

"I don't want to be a lot of trouble, but I'm hungry."

"I think we can scrounge up something for you to eat," Hearns stated as they walked out into the night air.

"What will it be, the food?" she asked. "I'm particular about what I eat."

"Then you get to choose," Stevens said and opened the door for her.

She looked concerned at Stevens. "What if it's something you don't like?"

"We're cops, we eat out a lot. We're not that particular."

She nodded her understanding of what made perfect sense.

Stevens shut the door, looked over the car to Hearns, smiled and shook her head.

He smiled, shrugged and playfully rolled his eyes.

Stevens laugh aloud as she slipped into the seat.

"What was so funny?" he asked as he buckled his seatbelt.

"I don't know." She looked directly ahead, past the windshield, into the night. "Suddenly I felt ..." she paused in thought, "complete, happy, being your partner and being a cop."

He steered the car out onto the street. "Yeah, me too."

Stevens glanced in the back and saw Amy Louise had slumped down in the seat and was asleep.

What an odd little girl, she thought.

Alton Duncan had dreaded every approaching moment on his journey to meet with Moreland and had even considered not passing along the message, but reconsidered.

He cautiously stepped from the helicopter and saw the escorts waiting.

Things were bad enough without taking a chance of making all worse, and he had no idea how to word the explanation of how such a simple task snowballed into an avalanche and determined he'd just have to jump in both feet and trust his instincts to do the rest.

He walked steadily, with confidence and flair. After all, he didn't get to this position in life without strong instincts and highly able talents, and he was only a step below Moreland himself. All things tallied, he imagined, it was bad, but not all that bad.

He nodded at the two and entered as they gestured. No greetings were exchanged and the three made their way into a room Alton had been in many times. The escorts stayed by the door as he made his way to the bar and poured a drink and took his seat in the large, dark brown, leather chair and had only settled in when Moreland entered.

Alton was relieved by Moreland's relaxed and friendly manner and stood as he walked in.

"We'll be fine, gentlemen," he said to the escorts and they left. He gestured to the chair where Alton had sat. "Go ahead, take your seat. I need a drink too."

He returned and sat on the sofa, placed the drink on a small table and eased back. "So, you had a nasty situation develop," he stated. "Tell me about it."

Alton, encouraged by the informal manner and tone, no code words, just two friends talking, relayed the circumstances, careful to provide as much detail as he remembered, step by step until the happening of that afternoon and evening. As he told of the small girl and all she'd done it was clear Moreland was no longer relaxed and had moved forward on the sofa.

"Tell me again, about this little girl, all that'd happened related to her."

Alton pondered over the best place to start and asked, "The things that happened today, or everything about the girl?

"The things that happened this evening," he stated as if it should've been obvious.

He recounted the events, slowly, with careful thought on the details and realized it probably sounded fabricated.

"This is incredibly hard to comprehend." Moreland now sat on the edge of the sofa. "She grabbed this man, Edwards, and he instantly died?" He shook his head. "How did he die?"

"He just died, it was almost instant."

"I mean, was he wounded, injured in someway, suffocated, what?"

Alton shrugged. "There were no obvious injuries, like I said, it happened very quickly. I can still see the calmness on his face. That's how fast it happened.

Moreland stood and paced. "This is impossible."

Alton noticed the odd tone, as one speaking of something familiar, not simply stated something to be impossible, but something of which he'd previously dreaded had impossibly occurred.

"This girl, you said she mentioned my name?"

"Yes, when she said she had a message for me to give to you."

He thought on this as he rubbed his chin and looked at Alton.

"What was the message?"

He felt foolish having to say it, but it had to be said. "We're coming."

"We're coming?"

"Yes, she said, tell Moreland, we're coming."

"We're coming." He incredulously repeated. "Who is this we?"

"That was part of the message."

"Well tell me the rest of it, you fool!" he yelled.

Alton cleared his throat and proceeded. "She said, when he asked who sent the message tell him: The sons of Seth."

Alton had no idea what that meant but instantly knew Moreland did. He saw it all over his face as it paled and his anger morphed deeper into disbelief.

"The sons of Seth." Moreland had not asked a question, nor made statement, but softly repeated what he'd just heard, as if only for his own benefit, having already grasped the significance. He returned to the sofa and sat in an extreme state of agitation, not agitated with anger but with worry.

Now Alton was worried. "What does this mean?"

"It means we need to be ready?"

"Get ready?"

"No, be ready."

"Then we should prepare," Alton stated with confidence, hoping for redemption in the eyes of Moreland and not understanding there was none to be had.

"There is nothing to prepare," Moreland said as he rose.

Alton stood and faced Moreland. "I don't understand."

"It's best you don't, not right now." He turned around, his back facing Alton. "Go ... go home, go away, go anywhere, make the best use of your time."

"But ..."

Moreland turned back to face Alton. "Go!"

Alton, confused, left.

⇥ ⇤

Kaye Fowler stepped into the house to find an upset and anxious husband.

"I had no idea where you were, what had happened to you ... nothing," Greg said.

"Something completely overwhelming and unexpected happened."

"Like what?" It sounded more like accusation. "Vigilante work?"

That caught her off guard and it was difficult to hide the disappointment and rising anger. "I'll explain later, it all happened so quickly I didn't have time to think, I'm still not settled down."

"I mean, that's it, you're just going to leave me hanging?"

Even after she'd told the story he was still upset and anxious. "It seems to me it would've come to your mind that there would be people worried, concerned."

She was in disbelief, after what she'd just told him and he's still prattling on that topic, like he didn't believe the story. She rose from the sofa. "I'm going to take a shower and go to bed."

"Don't you think we need to discuss this? I mean ..."

"Nothing more to discuss unless you want to discuss our marriage."

"I didn't know there was anything there to discuss."

She stopped and faced him. "Something happened tonight, something that I didn't tell you with the rest of it, something that'd be impossible for me to describe, I still don't fully understand it, and when I come home and find you waiting in whatever state you're in, it … it saddens me, but for you to listen to my account of things and still …"

He stopped her. "Maybe you need to go and take that shower, go to bed, rest the night and anything that needs to be discussed can be done when you're rested and in the right frame of mind."

"I think that's a good idea."

He watched her slowly walk the staircase, wondered if she had been out doing the type of things those detectives accused her of. He sat on a large overstuffed chair, in the quiet, thought about what it was she'd wanted to talk about concerning their marriage and imagined if she put it on the table to split up he'd jump at it.

He harbored the opinion she didn't appreciate him, his sacrifice of committing to a marriage with a partner loaded down with issues and baggage. He'd literally, in his mind, done her a favor by marrying her. He didn't like the idea of a divorce, of failing at something, of what his family and friends would think. Plus, he didn't really understand her and all her mysterious ways.

He was young and had plenty of time to start over, even if it required finding a new career, having hid the fact he didn't like the work or the company and had done it to please her. He'd also hid all the resentment that was building and maybe it was time to make changes. He'd sleep in the guest room to make a statement that he too could stand his ground and was not weak.

Upstairs, Kaye had no trouble falling asleep and woke rested, her mind light and clear. She felt like a child, free of those dark things that crept into the mind and dampen the spirit and drained the joy.

But there was one thing that did trouble her and needed to be done: To resolve everything with Greg.

Three days since her return home, Amy Louise sat with her family at the dinner table, stopped eating and looked at her dad. "May I visit Mr. Carroll?"

Bill stopped the fork before he could take a bite and thought a second. "When he's better he'll be going to prison." He hoped that ended it.

"I don't think a prison would be a nice place for you to visit," Linda said.

"I was thinking while he was at the hospital. That's something you could arrange since you're a Marshall, isn't it?"

She had him there.

"I could arrange that." He cleared his throat. "I'm just not sure it's a good idea."

She quietly sighed and returned to eating.

Bill started to return to eating, paused in thought again. "I'll see what I can do."

Her smile said it all, still she added, "Thank you."

This time she looked at Linda. "Mom, would you help me so that I could find and visit those kids who were at that place. I'd like to see them again."

"That might be difficult, finding out all that information."

"I'll help," Elaine said. "I'll find out the information."

"How will you do that?" Bill asked.

"I can find a lot of it online, on the computer."

"But some of this is confidential information, especially now, under these circumstances."

Amy Louise watched the exchange with interest.

"I know, but you'd be surprised the confidential stuff on the computer," Elaine stated.

"How do you know about confidential stuff on the computer?" Linda asked.

"From school, they were talking about the dangers of online theft and stuff like that."

Linda looked at Bill like it was news to her.

"She's right," Bill said. "It's a problem."

"You're a Marshall," Amy Louise said. "You could get that information easily."

Bill smiled and shook his head. "Yes, maybe I can, but it's not the right thing to do. You have to respect the rights of others to their privacy."

"I will get permission from their parents," she said. "I promise I'll not disrespect their privacy."

"Just why do you want to visit them?" Linda asked.

"They've been through some very bad things and it won't be easy for them to get better. I thought if I visited them it'd help."

That required no explanation, considering the miraculous and complete remission of Elaine's cancer.

"I'll see what I can do," Bill said.

"Thanks, Dad," Elaine said.

"Yes, thanks, Dad," Amy Louise added.

Elaine looked at Amy Louise and winked.

After some hard consideration, Kaye Fowler considered she might've been too hasty and decided to try to make the marriage work. But all was made moot when he filed for divorce. Several hours were spent in calm discussion on the matter of the future of their marriage. She suggested they set up meetings with Dr. Collier, work through the issues, but it was clear he'd made his mind up.

Greg gave four weeks notice and was given a nice check to provide a financial cushion until he could get another position. Kaye stepped into the vacated position and suggested to her dad they begin to seek someone for it, even if it meant hiring outside the company, which he rejected, determined to find someone inside. She knew his silent reasoning, that she would never jeopardize the company and would stay in the position as long as needed. He was correct in that reasoning.

Kaye followed her heart and her brain and made Clark Daniels aware of her intention for the future.

"I'm not putting you on the spot, Clark," she said and watched him take a big bite of pizza. "Just want you to know how I feel."

"I don't feel on the spot, and I know how you feel and I've felt the same way …"

She cut him off. "You've felt the same way? How long have you felt this way?"

"I was gonna say, if you'd give me time." He picked up a napkin, wiped the cheese off his chin. "When I first saw you there was something about you that caught my attention, I mean outside the fact of how pretty you are, but I'm not sure what that was that caught my attention.

"But you didn't say anything because I was married?"

"Yeah, that and then later when I found out I might not be living too much longer."

She looked down, momentarily avoided eye contact. "Well the married hurdle is out of the way, so what's your hold up? The health issue?"

"There's one other thing." He paused. "I'm afraid. Not afraid of dying, that's not it. I'm afraid of getting into something that is just too good to be true, if that makes any sense."

"Actually, it does. There was someone years back, he felt the same way, but he didn't say it in those words."

"And?"

"I'll tell you what I would've told him had I been given the chance: I see nothing about you or in you that causes me to believe that we can't last forever."

Emotion gripped him and he took a few seconds to gain composure. "What about the health deal? I mean I might not have much longer."

"I've got several things to say about that, Clark. One, you stop talking like you're dying and talk like your living, with plans and passion; two, no one knows how much time they have; three, what ever time we have I want to spend my time with you."

He struggled harder to hold his emotions in check, exhaled a large sigh, and said, "Well heck I might as well dive in head first … Kaye, why don't you and me get married."

"Now that's what I call a plan with passion." She laughed, and wiped away a tear as it ran down her cheek.

They both sat a few seconds in silence and absorbed the moment when she broke it. "You know, first chance we get, I've got a friend I'd like you to meet."

"Who'd that be?"

"A young girl. We've not been friends all that long, but I think she'd be someone you'd love."

"Then we need to make that happen, like you said, first chance we get." He took a sip from his drink. "What's her name?"

"Amy Louise Bradford."